EVE'S PARTY

Normally the old folk of Portlecombe love to spin a yarn. But mention 1936, and everyone clams up. Something bad happened back then. Something connected to the weird events of the last few days . . . Killer sharks in the bay. Dogs turned savage. Strange laughter in the hills . . . And Eve. Quiet, smiling, red-headed Eve. She's having a party. It's kind of a reunion. For anyone who survived her last one . . . Some stories are best left — buried.

Point Horror
UNLEASHED

EVE'S PARTY

Nick Turnbull

Complete and Unabridged

First published in Great Britain in 1999 by
Scholastic Children's Books
London

First Large Print Edition
published 2000
by arrangement with
Scholastic Children's Books
London

British Library CIP Data

Turnbull, Nick
Eve's party.—Large print ed.—
(Point horror)—Spectrum imprint
1. Horror tales
2. Young adult fiction
3. Large type books
I. Title
823.9′14 [J]

ISBN 0–7089–9516–0

Published by
F. A. Thorpe (Publishing)
Anstey, Leicestershire

Set by Words & Graphics Ltd.
Anstey, Leicestershire
Printed and bound in Great Britain by
T. J. International Ltd., Padstow, Cornwall

This book is printed on acid-free paper

To Judy, Scott, Bonnie and Kerry.
With love.

And to Ailsa,
whose party it really was . . .

1

They called him the Seal Man. Throughout the summer, he'd paddled along the edges of the South Devon coastline, his homemade canoe riding easily over the choppy, swirling surface of the sea. They said he lived in a caravan, somewhere behind Thurlestone Sands. Nobody really knew. Nor cared. Portlecombe was that kind of place.

Sometimes, as they left the harbour, heading for their lobster pots bobbling on the sea-bed off Start Point, the fishermen would wave, their shouts of 'Hello!' drifting across the waves. The man would smile, then wave back, briefly.

This afternoon, there were no fishermen.

He'd felt the first sting of the rain as it had started to spit from the low, grey clouds. The waves were now higher, more frequent, their dark, tumbling bodies fringed with a white, bubbling spume that flicked across their edges. The pair of grey seals he had been watching had long since disappeared into one of the many caves that the centuries had hacked into the hard granite of the cliffs.

Glancing over his shoulder, he could now see the darkening front of the coming storm, moving in slowly but surely from the open sea. He knew he wouldn't have time to make it back to the sands. Five minutes. Perhaps ten, at the most, before it hit him. His canoe had begun to yaw from side to side as the wind freshened and the waves sharpened.

In front of him, the cliffs rose sheer from the water's edge, reaching high into the sky where their jagged crown scratched a crazy line across the tumbling clouds. The rain was now harsher, more insistent. He had to land.

With an increasing sense of urgency, his arms now began to work the paddle more viciously, the blades at either side of the canoe biting into the cold, broken valleys of the sea as the waves now ran towards the shoreline rocks, only finally to hurl themselves against the pitiless, ragged stone. It would be a losing battle. Hard as he might try, he could not outrun the storm. Nor could he fight the increasing strength of the waves that were now pushing him gradually but inevitably toward the boiling edges of the shore.

Desperately now, his eyes searched the rocks. He swung the canoe round so that it now faced the land. Running with the waves, the light vessel began to cut through the water, its sharp bow first burying itself in the waves, then rearing like a frightened mare into the spray that whipped across their surface.

It was a gamble. The man knew he had to land. Already filling with water as the rain began to hammer down from the heavy skies above, the frail canoe would not last long in seas that were now grown angry. He could only hope, as the land grew closer, to find a break in the rocks. Painfully, he clawed the paddle deep into the water at one side. The canoe turned, skidding across the wave-top, dropping back as the wave ploughed on, before then being picked up by the next as its dark, curling face loomed behind him.

With each wave, the shore grew nearer, louder. Still he could see no break. Thrown against the pitiless face of the rocks, he would shatter like a china plate hurled against the sides of a quarry. Around him, the waves now boiled, sensing perhaps that they were close to their final, headlong charge toward their own destruction.

There was no break. Only the relentless, deafening crash of the water breaking over the rocks, the howl of the wind and the scream of the gulls as they swooped and span through the sweeping curtains of rain. The canoe reared up, almost falling back upon itself. Desperately, the man threw himself forwards, stopping the boat's somersault. As he did so, he dropped the paddle and, lying in the water on the floor of the boat, he looked back into the steepling waves behind him and saw it briefly arc into the air, almost as if in goodbye, before disappearing into the spray.

The boat rocked violently as the waves now picked it up and threw it brutally from side to side. The man gripped its sides, staring up into the merciless rain, screaming and then silent, as if in final supplication for a death that would be quick.

Then he felt the wave lift him. Higher than before, the final throw of the dice. It seemed to the man that he was being hoisted high into Heaven. In the driving, howling rain, and surrounded by the screaming gulls, he seemed to perch on the crest of the wave for ever, as if already dead and now safely cradled in eternity. Until, with sickening violence, the boat was suddenly wrenched and thrown down against the greedy clutches of the rocks.

Buried in the centre of the explosion of sound that followed, the man knew little of what happened. He'd expected the sudden, searing agony of his body being broken against the cliff, dragged and splintered like a rag doll against the unforgiving, granite teeth. Instead, there had been nothing. A sharp crack on the side of his head and then silence.

And now, he lay, floating, his feet treading water in what seemed to be a pool. His head hurt. From somewhere, a soft, grey light filtered through the gloom, whilst outside, the waves continued to thunder and beat against the walls of the cave.

And then he realized.

The wave that had thrown him against the cliff, rather than hurling him to his death, had thrown him into one of the seal caves. A one in a million chance. Perhaps more. He put his hand to the side of his head. It had been bleeding. He must have hit it on the side of the entrance.

Slowly, his eyes grew used to the dim light of the cave. Its roof was some ten or twelve feet above him, narrowing as it rose, its two sides meeting to form a line that ran back into the darker recesses of the cave. He kicked his feet and swam slowly towards the edge of the pool where a narrow path seemed to run along its side. Reaching it, he held on for a few moments and then carefully pulled himself up and out of the water. The noise he made echoed round the vaulted arches of the cave, a sharper sound now than the muffled threat of the seas beyond the cave's entrance.

He could see now that the cave stretched back far into the cliff. Oddly, there was no smell. No seals had used this cave. Nor any other animal.

He stood up, the heavy sea water falling from his clothes and dripping on to the stone beneath his feet. In the half-light, he began to edge forwards, at first with very short, careful steps. At his side, the waters of the pool were calm, a slight swell prompted only by the flurry of water at the cave's entrance. The pool seemed dark. It was almost certainly deep.

His breathing was heavy, painful. As he moved further into the cave, so the light began to falter. He stopped, wondering why he was walking away from the sea. The storm would subside. In time, the waves would calm and he would be safe to leave and somehow scramble along the shoreline to safety. And yet, he was walking on, almost as if he had been asked to. Almost as if he was the first man ever to have found this dark chamber and almost as if the spirits of time and therefore of the earth, needed to talk with him.

With his right hand, he felt his way along the wall. Still the stone path ran before him, a natural feature carved and modelled by the centuries. If anything, it seemed now to be growing wider. It was almost exactly where it widened sufficiently to become something of a platform that the man found it, hanging from a rusting nail hammered into the rock.

A small candle-lantern. A metal cage, dirty glass. The kind of lantern once in common use. Many years before.

The man stared at it, disbelieving at first. Then, slowly, almost as if expecting it to crumble in his hands, he reached up and took it carefully off the nail. He brought it down, his gaze running over the lamp's simple, almost crude, design. He turned it round. There was still a candle inside.

At its back, he found a small leather pouch hanging from the metal frame. He stooped, putting the lamp on the ground and then held the pouch closer to his face, studying it closely. At its neck, there was a short piece of string which snapped when he pulled at it. He let the pieces fall to the ground. Still the water echoed round the cave as it continued to fall from his clothes.

The pouch opened. Inside were several long, thin wooden sticks, darkened at one end. The man was puzzled and then realized what he was holding. Whoever had left the lamp here had left some matches with it.

He took one out and, bending down to the lamp again, he looked carefully at each of its sides until he found the glass panel that would slide out to allow access to the candle. He found it. He felt the candle. It was dry.

The first match broke as he scratched it

along the dry stone of the cave wall. So did the second. The third, however, sputtered into life and burnt for long enough to allow the man to push it slowly into the lamp and put it to the candle. It was a small flame at first but then, as the wax began to melt and the taper became more exposed, so the flame grew.

He straightened up, holding the lamp aloft. Now he could see deep into the cave, the light of the candle revealing that the path widened as it led to a small, high-ceilinged chamber. The waters of the pool splashed gently at its side. Slowly, he walked forwards again, his attention now taken by what seemed to be a stone box, laid on the floor of the chamber. The shadows thrown by the light of the lamp flickered along the walls as he moved. He stopped and listened. The sound of the seas outside had gone. Even the movement of the pool was silent. There was only the fall of water from his clothes. He coughed, letting the echoes die before moving once more towards the box.

He could see now that it was in two halves, the upper half acting as a lid. He thought it to be some five feet in length. Perhaps no more than two in height. He knelt beside it, putting the lamp on the ground where the light burned perfectly still. Deep in the cave, the air did not move.

There was no indication on the box of what it might be. It was man-made. That much was clear, for carved across its top was what appeared to be a snake. Other than that, it was featureless. The dust that had settled on it suggested that it had been where it was for a very long time. Like the lamp, thought the man.

He reached out to it, putting his hands at either side of the lid. Hesitating briefly, he then tried to move it, testing its weight. To his surprise, it seemed to move easily. Afraid of damaging it, however, he worked carefully, edging the lid off, inch by inch.

As he did so, he thought it odd that the candle flame had begun to flicker. Perhaps the air did move down here after all.

It took him some minutes before he was satisfied that he had moved it sufficiently to lift the lantern and look inside the stone box.

He stood up, picking up the lamp. The side of his head had begun to bleed again.

He slowly moved the light across to the box and, as he looked now at what was in

hurtled round a street corner only to collide with the unsuspecting boy. Neither of them had been hurt. The only damage done was to the box of eggs that Ben had been carrying and it had been an unlikely start to a friendship that had lasted throughout that summer and one which they had both been very happy to renew every holiday since then.

Ben didn't know too much about Lindsay's background. Only that she came from the North. That she went away to school. That her parents had split up. That she now spent most of her holidays with her grandfather, old Tom Walker.

He was standing on the quayside when Lindsay appeared. Below him, his brother's fishing boat was moored to the wooden landing steps that led down to the water. The tide was high.

'Morning.'

'Changed your mind?'

Lindsay nodded towards the boat as she walked up to him.

'About what?' said Ben.

'Helping Dan.'

'No, he's fine. And anyway, Ahab's going with him.'

As he spoke, he saw his brother appear

at the far side of the small harbour-side car-park, followed by a shorter man with a thick ginger beard.

'Is he really called Ahab?' said Lindsay.

'As far as I know.'

'Wasn't that the man who went off chasing Moby Dick?'

'Don't think so,' said Ben. 'I don't think he's that old.'

Dan Carson was older and taller than his brother. Several years of working the crabbing boats had thickened his neck and arms and, since he was rarely seen without stubble on his chin, he was known locally as 'Desperate'. His smile was broad and his skin tanned by the long summer days spent on the water.

'Hi, Ben. Lindsay.'

'Hi, Dan.'

'You want to change your mind about coming?'

Ahab had already gone down the steps to the boat and had disappeared into the small cabin that housed the steering wheel and provided simple shelter when the weather turned sour.

'Not today,' said Ben. 'Lindsay wants to take some photographs of bricks.'

'Sounds fun.'

Lindsay smiled at Dan. 'Ruins. And it's for a school project.'

'Even more fun.'

Below them, the boat's engine suddenly burst into life, roaring briefly as Ahab pulled the throttle back before allowing it to settle into its more familiar muffled pulse.

'Sounds like Ahab's in a hurry. Tell your grandad I was asking after him, Linds.'

'I will.'

She knew the Carsons and Walkers went back a long way.

Dan threw his duffel bag down on to the wide, curving deck of the Portlecombe 'crabber' below him, where Ahab was now untying the ropes that held it to the harbour wall. He paused as he walked down the wooden steps to the boat.

'Have a good time with the bricks.'

Moments later, the crabber was weaving its way carefully through the various boats that lay at anchor in the harbour. Ben watched it go and then turned to Lindsay.

'It's a long walk.'

'Doesn't matter. The sun's shining.'

* * *

Once clear of the harbour, Ahab now headed down the short estuary that led to the open sea beyond. On the beach to his left, he could see children playing at the edges of the water, others playing in the sand, their parents sitting beneath brightly coloured umbrellas. A flash of red amongst the rocks at one side caught his eye. Someone was standing there. A small girl. She seemed to be watching them go by.

'Ahab!'

Dan was shouting from the front of the boat, where he had been oiling the winch that would soon be hauling the crab pots up from the sea floor.

'Mind that boat!'

His attention taken by the beach, Ahab hadn't noticed the small sailing boat that was now heading straight for them. He pulled quickly on the lever to his right, throwing the boat into reverse and slowing it, allowing the small dinghy to pass by in front.

'You missed them!' shouted Dan, smiling.

Ahab stuck his head out of the wheelhouse window, a broad grin on his face.

'Just practisin'.'

Dan watched the small boat sail by, keeling slightly in the breeze. There were two people in it. One waved. He waved back, listening to the growl of the diesel engine as the fishing boat once more moved forwards, picking up speed. He wondered if they'd noticed the shark's fin cutting through the water some fifty yards behind them.

'There's been a few of them about this summer,' he said, walking back to join Ahab.

'Just a basking shark,' said Ahab. 'Won't hurt nobody.' He swung the wheel gently to his left.

As the boat drew closer, the fish disappeared beneath the surface of the water. Ahab slowed and then finally cut the engine, allowing the boat to drift. Leaning over the side of the boat, they could clearly see the dark shadow of the creature swimming slowly below them.

'It's big,' said Ahab.

He started the engine again, heading for the Greystone Rocks that marked the entrance to the estuary. Once safely past them, Ahab opened the throttle to full speed as the boat now moved into the open sea.

As they did so, unseen, the fish behind them had now turned and was following.

* * *

It took them almost an hour to walk to Lindsay's 'pile of bricks'. In the heat of the morning sun it had been hard work, and by the time they reached the old gates that sat at the top of the driveway, they were both grateful for the two bottles of water Ben had been carrying in his shoulderbag.

'Is this it?' said Lindsay, sitting on the ground and leaning back against one of the peeling gateposts.

'No. These are just the gates.'

Lindsay smiled.

'OK.'

Ben pointed beyond the gates. Thick overhead with the branches of trees that had grown and become entangled, a muddy track led downhill, curling finally to the left and disappearing behind a group of tall pine trees.

'There's not much of it left,' said Ben. 'I mean, I don't know what sort of ruins you're looking for.'

'Any old ruins,' said Lindsay. 'Preferably with a ghost.'

Ben laughed.

'I don't think they come out in the daytime.'

Finishing their water, they started walking down the sloping driveway. As they walked, so it felt cooler. The trees above blocked the sunlight. A breeze seemed to blow up towards them. After the heat of the earlier walk, it was refreshing.

'What happened to it?' said Lindsay.

'It burnt down,' said Ben.

'When?'

'Oh, I don't know. Years ago.'

'And they never tried to rebuild it?'

'No. To be honest, I don't think many people even know it's here. You'll never hear anybody talk about it in the village.'

They had reached the pines.

* * *

The sea was calm. Almost flat. In the distance, they could see the short stubby flags floating on the surface that told where the first string of pots were lying. Some two miles out from the shore, they were alone, the only sound — apart from the steady rhythm of the Perkins diesel beneath the deck — being the occasional gull's cry as the birds circled high above.

The flags were nearer now. Ahab slowed the engine.

'Fingers crossed,' said Dan, walking forwards towards the winch.

It hadn't been a good year for the Portlecombe fishermen and Dan had almost become used to pulling up a string of a dozen pots, only to find nothing in them.

Ahab waited until the flags were no more than ten or twelve metres away and then cut the engine, letting the boat drift slowly in towards them. Leaning over the side of the boat, Dan had a long metal hook in his hands which, as they drew alongside the first flag, he swung into the water, catching the rope that dropped down towards the seabed from the base of the flag. Pulling it up, he looped it over the drum of the winch and fastened it to the hoop which was bolted into the wooden planking of the deck. Turning the handle on the side of the winch, he then wound in the initial slack of the line that disappeared down into the depths of the ocean, until, as it tightened, contact was made with the first pot.

Ahab had left the small wheelhouse and was standing on the deck, gazing out over the flat sea. The wind had died away. Dan had started the small electric winch-motor which was now humming quietly as the pots were slowly pulled to the surface. The heat from the sun was fierce. In the distance, where the shoreline should have been, a haze had settled, turning the line of cliffs into a narrow, smudged margin at the bottom of the sky. The boat rocked slightly, shaken by the movement of the pots on the other end of the line.

Ahab found himself watching the surface of the sea some thirty yards to his left. There, a small cormorant was floating on the water, paddling lazily, dipping its head every so often, as if drinking. The bird was also suffering from the heat.

The dorsal fin appeared first, followed quickly by the smaller tail fin, as the fish came to the surface. Surprised, the cormorant shook its wings and with a short cry, lifted itself into the air, flying quickly away to the south. Ahab watched as the two fins slowly cut through the water. Looking at the distance between them, he thought the shark was probably some fifteen feet long. And it wasn't a basking shark.

'Dan.'

'Yeah?'

Dan looked across the boat.

'Have a look at this.'

'What?'

'Over there. In the water.'

Ahab pointed to the fins which were now beginning a wide circle around the boat.

'What is it?'

'I think it's a mako,' said Ahab. 'But I've never seen one that size.'

As he spoke, the two fins slowly sank back beneath the surface and the fish was gone.

⋆ ⋆ ⋆

They turned the bend by the pine trees and then stopped. At first neither of them spoke. In front of them, now almost entirely overgrown with ivy; with grasses; with brambles, were the crumbling, broken walls of what had obviously once been a large house.

The roof had long gone, charred stumps of timber being all that remained of its rafters. The windows were no more than holes in the walls. Where the large front doors had once hung, there was now simply a wide opening through which the decaying interior of the house could be glimpsed.

Standing quietly, almost peacefully, in the sunlight, it reminded Lindsay of a doll's house, whose childish owner had thrown a tantrum, stamped on it and left it to rot at the bottom of the garden.

'I told you there wasn't much left of it,' said Ben, as they started walking again.

'It's fine,' said Lindsay, taking her camera out of its leather case. 'And it looks really weird.'

'Is that good?'

'Absolutely.'

She stopped, lifting her camera up to her eye and pointing it at the house. The shutter clicked. She smiled.

'You know, it's odd,' she said, 'but if you listen carefully, it's almost as if you can hear the sounds of children playing.'

As they walked up to the house, Lindsay took more photographs. The slight breeze had died and the sun was now high, bathing the ruins in a harsh, glaring light. But it was only as they began to walk round to the side of the house, following the track of what had once been a garden path, that Ben realized what was wrong.

'Linds.'

'Yeah?'

'Have you noticed something?'

'Like what?'

'The sun's shining. Right?'

'Right.'

'So why does it feel so cold?'

⋆ ⋆ ⋆

The first string of pots had brought them three crabs, which now sat twitching at the bottom of a large tea chest, lashed to the side of the wheelhouse. There had been none in the second and, as they now approached the third, Dan was beginning to wonder when, or even if, their luck was going to change.

'OK Ahab! That's fine!'

Without turning to look at the wheelhouse, Dan was shouting as the boat approached the third set of flags. Ahab hadn't heard him. Nor had he seen him. He was too busy scanning the surface of the sea around them.

'Ahab!'

Suddenly realizing what was happening, for the second time that morning, Ahab had to make a sudden grab for the lever to his right to put the boat into reverse. He wasn't quick enough. The bows of the crabber had already run over the flags and they were now bouncing along the underside of the boat's keel.

'Cut the engine!' yelled Dan. 'They'll foul up round the propeller!'

Ahab reached for the ignition key and flipped it to one side. The Perkins stopped. The propeller slowed but the momentum of the boat meant that the flags still worked their way down its length. As they reached the turning propeller, they were sucked towards it, finally twisting themselves around it. Now it stopped.

The boat drifted silently on the flat surface of the sea. Beneath it, the line ran away to the pots lying on the sea-floor.

'Sorry,' said Ahab. 'I was . . . '

'Doesn't matter,' said Dan, leaning over the back of the boat and peering down into the water. 'I don't think it's too serious.' He stood back and pulled his shirt off.

'Fine time for sunbathing,' said Ahab.

Dan smiled.

'There's a knife in the wheelhouse.'

'Dan, I'm not so sure . . . '

'Ahab, if we don't cut that line off the propeller, we're going to be stuck out here all day.'

Ahab shrugged his shoulders and stepped back into the wheelhouse. He reappeared moments later and handed Dan a broad-bladed fish-knife. Dan took it and, dropping his shirt on to the deck, he climbed over the side of the boat and lowered himself into the still, blue water. Slowly, he swam round towards the propeller and, putting his head below the water's surface, he could see the rope twisted round the gleaming brass shaft. The flags were floating at one side, still fastened to the rope. Taking a deep breath, Dan sank beneath the water, first cutting the flags free with swift, sawing strokes of the knife.

Leaning over the back of the boat, Ahab watched him. He saw the flags bob up to the surface and then drift slowly away, carried by a gentle tide. The bright sun high above meant that he could see clearly into the depths below him. To his right, he could hear a small group of gulls calling to each other as they circled lazily on the warm air currents. He turned to watch them for a moment.

A sudden splashing in the water below made him turn back. Quickly. It had been Dan coming up for air, his lungs bursting.

'You done it?'

Ahab's voice was hurried.

'Not yet,' gasped Dan, wiping the salt water from his face. 'Here, grab this.'

He held up the newly-cut end of the line that stretched down to the pots below. Ahab leant over, taking the line from him.

'Try and get it wrapped round the winch. I don't want to lose the pots.'

'How much more have you got to do?'

'Not a lot.'

Dan disappeared below the surface again. Holding the line, Ahab worked his way across the deck and, reaching the winch, began to wind it round the thick metal drum. As he did so, out of the corner of his eye, he noticed a slight movement on the sea's surface. He stopped winding, staring intently at the water, breathing hard. He could hear nothing. The gulls had gone.

For several moments, he held himself perfectly still, watching.

He knew there had been something there. He'd been working the boats for far too long not to understand every twitch of the sea, every shade, every pattern, every colour.

Slowly, his eyes still staring at the water, he began to shuffle quietly across the deck, almost as if not to disturb whatever it was that was now below the water. Then he moved more quickly, the panic beginning to take over.

'Dan!'

He turned, stumbled across a rope lying on the deck, crashed against the side of the wheelhouse.

'Dan! Dan!'

He pulled himself up and hurled himself against the back of the boat, clutching at the rail, hanging almost impossibly out over the water and now screaming.

'Dan! Get out!'

Below him, he could see Dan's body, his legs kicking slightly, his arm moving backwards and forwards as he cut at the rope on the propeller.

'Dan! It's back! Get out!'

He glanced across the water. Still nothing.

Dan broke the surface.

'Grab my hand! Now!' Ahab was screaming. 'Dan!'

'What's the — '

Through the still, clear water, Ahab could see the long, dark shape of the fish as it now climbed from the depths towards them.

Dan waved his arm in the air. Ahab grabbed it, both hands fastening to it like claws, every muscle in his body in agony as he struggled to haul the fisherman out of the water. Dan grasped the side of the boat with his other hand and pulled. And then he looked down.

The shark was closing on him quickly, its outline now clearly visible as it powered up through the silent water.

'Help!'

His body scored through with pain, Ahab screamed again as, with one final despairing effort, he wrenched Dan's body over the back of the boat. Bursting out of the water, its eyes closed as it attacked, the shark's head suddenly reared above them. The fishermen clung to the side of the wheelhouse, helpless and screaming as the huge, white-gummed jaws of the fish yawned wide before closing on the wooden planking of the boat, splintering it as the creature fell back into the water. The sea boiled, cascading high into the air, showering the men and the boat which was rocking violently, threatening to overturn.

And then all was silent.

The surface of the sea calmed. The movement of the boat slowed. The shark did not return.

* * *

It was the laughter of a child. It was unmistakable. A young girl. A short, piercing, bubbling laugh that they both heard. And yet, there was no one to be seen.

'Maybe it was some kind of animal,' said Lindsay. They had stopped on the track leading away from the house. They listened intently, wondering if they would hear the sound again.

'Animal?' said Ben.

'A sheep. Or a goat or something.'

'Can you see any sheep or goats anywhere?'

Lindsay turned to look at him. 'No. But then I can't see any children either.'

Ben looked back at her. And then past her. 'Look!'

'What?'

'Behind you! Look!'

Lindsay turned sharply round. A tangled garden. Overgrown bushes. Tall firs. Low, sweeping willows. Nothing more.

'What am I looking at?'

'She's gone.' Ben's words were slow, halting.

Lindsay turned back to look at him again. He had visibly paled. A vein in his neck was pulsing hard.

'Who's gone?'

'The girl,' said Ben. 'There was a girl . . . standing. Just there.'

And he pointed towards the silhouette of a tall, thin rowan tree that stood against the sunlight, the fingers of its branches moving slowly in a gentle midday wind.

3

It was almost dark by the time Tom Walker began to approach the churchyard. The last, long traces of the evening sun were now no more than flickers at the edges of the horizon and, as he looked up into the darkening skies above him, Tom could see the first stars of the night beginning to appear. He remembered his mother telling him that the tiny pinpricks of light were fairies carrying lanterns to the moon. He smiled at the memory.

The night air was warm and he walked slowly. St Peter's was on a hillside, overlooking the small Portlecombe harbour. When it had first been built, in the mid-nineteenth century, the village had been almost entirely dependent on the sea. So it had seemed only fitting that God's house should have been sited where He could watch over the fishermen and their boats.

These days, the harbour was more likely to be filled with pleasure boats and sailing dinghies. Not that they were necessarily a bad thing, in Tom's view, whenever the subject of holiday-makers came up as he and his friends sat on the quayside, talking of days long gone by. Nothing would ever stop the world from changing and it was, anyway, much easier for the townspeople to make money out of the summer visitors than it was to earn money from the sea.

One or two of the other old men would disagree but, in their hearts, they knew Tom was right. The old ways were going, just as the countryside itself was being slowly whittled away by the motor car and the developer.

Tom could see the outline of the church now. He knew that it had been in the churchyard, all those years ago, that the families had gathered. Perhaps that was why Donald had suggested meeting there this evening. That, and the certainty that no one would hear their conversation.

He hoped that Donald would already be there. The idea of standing alone in a churchyard, lit only by the pale light of the half-moon above, did not appeal to him. As children, they had always known that it was where the spirits of long-dead villagers danced among the gravestones and, even if Tom, in his old age, had long since grown out of such fantasies, it is in old age that the memories and impressions of childhood are most often recalled. He reached the small, wooden, churchyard gate.

'Donald?'

He called out softly, listening for his friend's reply.

'That you, Tom?'

A figure stepped out from the shadows of the large oak tree that guarded the church and the many souls buried in the earth beside it.

'You been here long?' said Tom, thinking of his own fears a few moments earlier.

'No,' said Donald. 'Not long.'

Below them, the bright lights of the quayside restaurants glittered and cars wound their way through the stubby, small streets behind them. Somewhere, a motor launch chugged its way across the darkened waters of the harbour. Someone was shouting, their muffled voice echoing across the water.

'It's warm,' said Tom.

Around them, the crickets of the hillside were chattering, their high-pitched chorus either a conversation or a warning of the predatory night-jar.

Donald had taken a pipe from his pocket.

'You've heard, have you?' he said.

'Yes,' said Tom. 'I have.'

'What do you think?'

Tom watched as the flame of his match briefly lit Donald's face as he lit his pipe. His eyes were worried.

'How's Dan?' said Tom, softly.

'He'll live.' Donald sucked deeply on his pipe, blowing smoke into the night-time air. 'Just as well he had that fool Ahab with him.'

'Ahab's all right,' said Tom

'He's a fool. And his father before him.'

'Seems he saved Dan's life.'

Donald Carson grunted. That much was true. If it hadn't been for Ahab, his grandson would now be dead.

'Was it really a shark?' said Tom.

Donald nodded. 'They both said so.'

Tom turned, looking again over the harbour towards the dimmed outline of the cliffs and the sea beyond. He hadn't mentioned Ben or Lindsay. Or what Ben had seen. Now, as he stood gazing into the night, almost as if looking back in time, he knew that his worst fears were true.

'So,' said Donald, taking the pipe out of

his mouth and looking steadily at his friend. 'What do you think?'

Tom turned to look at him. He spoke quietly.

'I think she's back.'

4

Ben's father was kneeling under the boat, looking up at its keel. From time to time he prodded the wooden planking with a short iron bar, feeling for any weaknesses in the structure. Much of the back of the boat had disintegrated but, hopefully, the rest could be saved. 'Your brother was lucky,' he said, finally crawling out and walking round to join Ben, who was standing in the middle of the boatyard running his eyes over the damage done by the shark.

'You're not kidding,' said Ben.

It was possible, just, to make out the rough semi-circle cut through the wood by the fish's teeth, and it didn't take a lot of imagination to work out what would have happened to Dan if he had been left in the water.

'You ever seen anything like it?'

His father shook his head.

'No.' He took his cap off and rubbed it across his brow. Rain had been forecast but as yet, in the early afternoon, the sun was still burning down from the sky.

'They say there's been one before.'

'A shark attack?'

'A long time ago. One of the old men down by the quayside was talking about it. Not that he said very much.'

His father smiled. 'If I had five pounds for every story those old duffers carry round in their heads, I'd be a very rich man. But, as it happens, I'm just a simple boat-builder.'

'With the very simple problem of patching up a shark bite,' grinned Ben. 'I'll see you this evening.' He turned and began to walk across the yard, picking up a short piece of wood on his way. It would do to throw for his gran's dog.

'Where are you going? Your mum will want to know.'

Ben looked back briefly. 'She already does. Gran's.'

'What for?'

'Don't ask me. It's all to do with this project of Lindsay's. I sometimes wish I'd never offered to help.'

'I don't believe that,' said his father, smiling.

'And mind you don't run into any more ghostly children.'

Ben laughed. He knew his father hadn't believed his story. He was beginning to think he didn't even believe it himself any longer. But then, he thought, as he wandered out of the yard, who would have believed that a shark would try to kill his brother?

* * *

Phoebe Stone had been born in 1926, less than half a mile away from where she now lived, on the edges of Shadycombe Creek, a quiet backwater that ran from the Portlecombe harbour and twisted its way inland.

Hers was one of several small, white-washed cottages, although it stood at some distance from the others, being closer to the creek itself. Her neighbours, it seemed, preferred to be further up the hill. Beside the cottage, a stooping willow tree dropped its branches into the slow-moving water which was drained away each day by the tide to reveal a shallow basin of deep brown mud. A small garden ran round her home which, in spring, was a rich mass of colour as the bluebells, daffodils and primroses that had slept all winter now finally burst from the ground.

Phoebe had grown up in Portlecombe and, apart from a brief spell in the mountains of North Wales at the beginning of the war, she'd lived in the area all her life. Her husband had been a local man, a carpenter called William Stone, who'd been killed on the beaches of Normandy. Their daughter, Dorothy, had been born in that same year and had grown up in the Shadycombe cottage, living there until, at the age of twenty-three, she too was married and left home.

'Not that she went very far,' said Ben, as he and Lindsay walked along the side of the creek. 'My dad had a flat above his boat-yard on the harbour-front and that's where they lived when they first got married.'

'It's a nice name, isn't it?' said Lindsay.

'What?'

'Phoebe.'

'Well, in that case it suits her,' smiled Ben. They walked on in silence for a while. The heat had become oppressive. Already, they had heard two or three distant rumbles of thunder. Perhaps when it came, the storm would clear the air.

'A penny for them,' said Lindsay.

'For what?' Ben looked at her.

'Your thoughts. A penny for your thoughts. It's a saying.'

Ben smiled and shrugged his shoulders. 'I don't know . . . it's just . . . Lindsay.' Ben had stopped smiling. 'Do you believe me? That I saw that girl.'

Lindsay didn't reply at first. 'I don't know, Ben. What I do believe is that you think you saw her.'

'But she was there.'

'You think she was there. Maybe it was like one of those times in the desert. You know, when people think they've seen an oasis. Only it isn't there.'

'A mirage?'

'Something like that.'

'Maybe.'

They could now see the small cottages of Shadycombe, Ben's grandmother's standing on its own beside the willow. Lindsay thought it looked lonely.

'Are you sure she doesn't mind?' she said, as they reached the small wicker gate by the roadside..

'I'm sure she doesn't,' said Ben. 'Anyway, she likes having visitors.'

The gate clicked as he opened it. Almost immediately, a dog started barking. A loud, compelling bark that suggested it was a large dog.

'What's that?' said Lindsay.

'That's Edison.'

Moments later, a tall, dark alsatian came bounding from the cottage, escaping as an elderly lady opened the front door. Within two or three strides, it was with them, barking. Instinctively, Lindsay stepped back.

'Shut up, Edison,' laughed Ben. He leant forwards, stretching out his arm and ruffling the fur on the dog's head. It calmed the animal. Ben straightened up again, smiling as the old woman joined them.

'Gran. Meet Lindsay.'

* * *

They sat in the small lounge at the back of the house, which looked out over the creek. Ben had been right. His grandmother did enjoy having visitors.

Within minutes of their arrival, she had boiled the kettle and served up a broad plate of home-cooked scones. She was delighted to be able to help Lindsay with her project.

'Images Of Yesterday'. Phoebe had thought it an odd title but if it gave her an excuse to sit back and take a trip down memory lane, then she was only too pleased to do so. Hers had been a happy life. Apart from the early death of her husband.

When she had received the brown envelope that brought the news of the death of Lance-Corporal William Stone, she had stored it carefully away in her bedside drawer and vowed that his memory would never be forgotten. Which was why, in each room of the cottage, there was at least one picture of him. In the small lounge, he sat now above the brick fireplace, staring quietly from a gold-edged frame as Phoebe talked, her mind wandering back through the years.

Outside, dark clouds of the coming storm had gathered, masking the sun completely and darkening the afternoon. A wind had sprung up, shifting the branches of the nearby willow and rattling a small window behind Lindsay's head. Phoebe paused and started to pull herself out of the chair.

'I'd better . . . '

'No, I'll do it,' said Lindsay, getting

quickly to her feet. She turned and stepped across to the window. Already, the first spots of rain were slowly jinking their way down the panes of glass. She could hear Phoebe switching on the small light beside her chair. She was offering Ben another cup of tea, only then to discover that there was none left in the pot.

As Lindsay reached the window, she heard another peal of thunder, now very much closer. Outside, it was almost dark and she stared out towards the creek, where the waterside reeds played in the wind, like so many shadows. It was only because the dog moved slightly that she noticed it. It was standing on the short path that led down to the creek, its back to the water and its head turned towards the cottage. It was now quite still again. Its front legs straight, the large triangle of its head unmoving. It was staring at Lindsay. For a moment she stared back and then she turned quickly away, shutting the small window with a bang.

'Sorry, I . . . '

'Don't worry,' said Phoebe. 'It's had worse treatment than that over the years.'

'It's just that . . . '

'Yes?'

Lindsay shook her head. And then smiled. 'It doesn't matter. It's nothing.'

The rain began to fall with the first crack of thunder overhead.

* * *

It had been raining for nearly a quarter of an hour when Phoebe went into the kitchen to put the kettle on again. It hammered against the windows and drummed on the slate roof above. Often, high above, the thunder would roll across the Portlecombe hills, before finally exploding with a fury that seemed to shake the very foundations of the buildings themselves.

Phoebe reached the sink, turning the tap and letting the cold water run into the empty kettle. The kettle filled. Gently, she took it away, turning the tap off. Setting it down on one side, she plugged in the electric lead. The small red light flickered into life as she switched it on. And then she waited, listening for the first sounds of the water bubbling.

Watched pot never boils, she thought, and busied herself clearing some of the washing-up out of the sink.

As she worked, she glanced from time to time through the small kitchen windows in front of her. Every so often, the lightning would bathe the garden outside in sudden, brilliant light. For that moment, every detail could be seen. The grass. The trees. The hedge that ran alongside the waters of the creek.

The kettle was beginning to boil. Once again, the thunder crashed overhead. Almost immediately, the lightning flickered savagely across the sky and, in that brief moment of brilliant illumination, standing on the grass, Phoebe Stone saw someone she had hoped never to see again in her life.

* * *

They heard the scream. And then the squeal of the wooden kitchen chairs and the breaking of wood as the old woman's body fell over them.

'Gran!'

Shouting, Ben threw himself from his chair and across the small room. The thunder burst above them. The rain hammered against the cottage, almost as if trying to drive its way through the stubby walls. Inside the kitchen, Phoebe was lying on the floor, her body angled, and blood from a deep cut on the side of her head seeping on to the cold, stone floor.

'Gran! Say something!' Ben was kneeling beside the old woman, shaking her.

'Lindsay — the phone! Get an ambulance!' He thought he saw the old woman's eyes flicker. 'Lindsay!'

But Lindsay hadn't moved. She was standing quite still in the kitchen doorway, her face white, her dark eyes staring across the room past Ben. Again, the thunder crashed overhead. The small kitchen light hanging from the ceiling swung violently from side to side.

'Lindsay!'

'Ben . . . '

When Lindsay spoke, it was in quiet, hushed tones, almost as if she was afraid of being overheard.

'What?'

'Look . . . '

Her eyes hadn't moved as she had spoken, fixed on whatever she had seen.

'At the window.'

Ben slowly turned his head away from her, his eyes moving slowly round the room. The rain hissed and spat at the glass of the windows and yet it seemed, suddenly, as if the room had fallen silent. There was a part of him that did not dare to look. A part of him that already knew what was there. A chill ran through his body. His throat tightened. And then, at last, he saw her. There, her face pressed across the window, lashed by the rain, was the young girl. Smiling.

* * *

'Out! Come out! Whatever you are!'

He was shouting. Screaming. His clothes soaked by the vicious, unrelenting rain falling from a blackened sky, Ben ran from one shadow to another, a broken chair-leg in one hand. The light from the kitchen window spread feebly across the lawn.

The girl had gone.

By the side of the creek, Ben stopped. He looked along the banks, now shrouded in a curtain of rain. The branches of the willow tree were flinging themselves about in crazy, exaggerated patterns, like the hands and fingers of an excited pianist.

He looked back towards the cottage. He had left the door open and now Lindsay was standing there, waiting. She seemed to be shouting something but her words were lost in the rain. Ben thought he might have heard the word 'hospital'. In his panic, hurling open the back door and rushing blindly out into the storm in search of the girl, he had briefly forgotten his grandmother.

He turned and began to walk back towards the cottage. Halfway there, he stopped. There had been a movement. He was sure of it. To his right. Tightening his grip on the wooden chair-leg, he moved slowly towards the small garden shed, peering into the gloom. The thunder rumbled again but this time further away. The storm was easing.

Quite suddenly, the dog was in front of him. Almost as if it had appeared from nowhere. It was standing quite still, watching him, the rain bouncing from the animal's shining, matted fur.

Ben smiled.

'Edison.'

He took a step forward. The dog snarled, its lips curling back, revealing dull, thick teeth.

'What . . . ?'

Ben stiffened. There was a strange,

haunted look about the creature. A wildness in its eyes. Its hackles were raised. A low growl came from its throat. Ben edged away, slowly. The dog watched him. Still the rain fell, hissing into the ground. The cottage was not far away. Twenty metres. Twenty-five. Ben wasn't sure. But he knew that he had to try. Again, the dog growled, a long, cruel sound that grew louder as Ben moved back. It seemed now to be leaning back on its hind legs. Ben knew that it was about to spring. He turned and ran.

With a howl, the dog leapt forward. The ground was wet. Ben's feet slipped as he ran over the grass. Ahead, the light at the doorway was now no more than a blur.

'Run! Ben!'

Lindsay was screaming. With a howl, the dog hurled itself towards Ben, its jaws closing on his lower leg. He felt the pain knife through his body. Falling, tumbling, turning, he lashed out wildly with the chair-leg, hitting the head and body of the creature. It released its jaws, briefly stunned. It was enough. With no sense of the pain, Ben scrambled to his feet and stumbled desperately through the rain toward the safety of the door. Reaching it, he fell into the hallway as Lindsay slammed it shut, screaming as the dog hurled itself against it. She jammed the bolt into its socket and slowly slipped to the ground, tears coursing down her face.

* * *

They sat on the kitchen floor. The old woman was breathing hard, her eyes still closed, her body still stretched out where she had fallen.

'Ben.'

Lindsay's voice was hoarse. Trembling. Ben looked at her.

'Ben. What's happening?'

Ben's eyes turned again to the window. The rain was lighter now and the drops slid more slowly down the glass. He shook his head as he spoke.

'I don't know.'

In the distance, they could hear the sound of a siren. The wind had died now and, in the east, the skies were beginning to brighten.

5

Ben was sitting at the edge of the bed. He'd been there for just over two hours, waiting for the old woman to wake. Her breathing was heavy. The drugs they had given her had obviously put her into a very deep sleep.

Ben didn't like hospitals. There was always that strange, antiseptic smell that seemed to seep into your clothes. Long, echoing corridors where everyone walked hurriedly backwards and forwards, whispering to each other. Patients being wheeled around on trolleys, unsmiling, staring upwards at the ceiling. And ugly, almost sinister objects such as the bottle hanging above his grandmother's bed. A long, plastic tube dangled from it, the other end of which was stuck in his grandmother's arm.

Ben looked up from his book.

Hidden from the rest of the hospital ward by the curtain that circled the bed, he couldn't see what was happening but the noises suggested that some kind of meal was being served. The squeaking wheels of the trolley. The muffled, brief conversations. The sound of trays being settled and water poured.

He glanced at his watch. Half past twelve.

The curtains behind him parted. Turning in his chair, Ben half expected to see a chef's head appearing. It was the doctor. He smiled briefly.

'Any news?'

Ben shook his head. 'No. I'm afraid not.'

The doctor moved to the top of the bed where Phoebe's heavily-bandaged head lay back against the stiff white pillows.

'A nasty knock. Bad enough at any age but when you're . . . ' The doctor paused. 'Do you know how old she is?'

'Seventy-eight.' Ben remembered the party they'd had for her, earlier in the summer when she'd promised to live to be a hundred-and-two. And now here she was, lying unconscious in a hospital bed.

'Is she going to be all right?'

The doctor had taken a thermometer out of his top pocket and was pushing it gently into the old woman's mouth, where he then held it.

'I think so.'

'You think so?'

'Nothing can be certain. Not until she wakes up.'

'When's that going to be?'

'I don't know.' The doctor watched the old woman carefully. 'Soon, I hope.'

* * *

Ben stayed with his grandmother for much of the afternoon. His father had called in for a short while, leaving a bunch of grapes and some flowers when he left. He hadn't believed the story about the little girl. And, as far as he was concerned, the dog had simply been driven briefly mad by the storm. It happened sometimes.

As he sat by the bed, his book now lying on the floor beside him, Ben let his mind wander back over the previous afternoon. There had been a storm. Just as there had been a face at the window. And this time, Lindsay had seen her. He didn't know how she'd managed to disappear. Or why the dog had suddenly attacked him. Maybe his father was right. Maybe it had been no more than the storm. But the storm had nothing to do with the face. Storms don't conjure up faces. The girl had been there.

His grandmother moved slightly, her left arm shifting across the blankets.

'Gran?'

Ben's voice was gentle.

There was no reply. The old woman seemed to still be sleeping. Ben watched her carefully for some moments and then scribbled a brief note on the notepad the doctor had given him. Then he sat back again. He wondered briefly if his grandmother would mind if he had some of her grapes. His mind started to drift again. This time to the house. The ruins where he had first seen the girl. Where it had been cold even though the sun had shone. Where they had heard the laughter.

'I don't want . . .'

Ben suddenly stiffened in his chair. The words had been his grandmother's. And yet her eyes were still closed. She was speaking softly, slowly.

'I don't . . .'

'Gran?' She was mumbling. Ben couldn't distinguish the words. He bent forwards. 'Gran?'

'I don't want to . . . '

'You don't want to what, Gran? What don't you want to do?'

'I don't want to go to the party!'

Suddenly, the old woman was shrieking. She was sitting bolt upright in her bed, her eyes wide open, staring wildly ahead of her. Sweat covered her face.

'Gran!'

'I don't want to go!'

Her voice was shrill. Piercing. She was screaming as if in the grip of some terrible nightmare. Her eyes were open but unseeing.

'Gran!'

The curtains were suddenly thrown back. A nurse appeared, moving quickly to the screaming woman, wrapping her arms around her, trying to push her back down to the pillow again.

'Tell them I'm not going!'

There was a voice at the heart of the scream that Ben recognized. The voice of fear.

And then, as suddenly as it had appeared, the fit was past. The old woman's body fell limp in the nurse's arms. She was breathing very quickly. Above her head, the glass bottle swung backwards and forwards, the tube dangling loosely from it, now ripped out of Phoebe Stone's arm.

* * *

'Did she say anything about the party?'

His father swung the Land Rover out to the right, overtaking a tractor grinding out its way home along the narrow Devonshire lane.

'Nothing,' said Ben. 'She just kept on screaming that she didn't want to go.'

They drove on in silence for a while. There had been little point in staying on at the hospital. Ben's grandmother had been heavily sedated and they had left her sleeping peacefully.

'I hope she doesn't get those nightmares again,' said Ben, as they reached the small village of Charlborough. In the distance, he could see the cliffs and the headland that marked the entrance to Portlecombe's estuary and harbour.

'They said it was a freak.'

They moved slowly through the village towards the rolling green and golden fields of the countryside beyond. And, as they left the small houses behind them, Ben watched as the roadside hedgerows began to flicker by once more.

'Dad.'

'Yes?'

'What are we going to do about the dog?'

'What dog? Edison?'

'Yes.'

'Nothing. It's not even ours.'

'But it might attack her.'

'I doubt it. What happened to you was a freak. Like your gran's nightmare.'

'Dad, that thing was trying to kill me.'

'Don't be ridiculous.'

'Just like that shark and Dan.'

John Carson had already made that connection for himself but the last thing he was going to do was suggest it to Ben. He didn't understand it any more than his son but then maybe there was nothing to understand. Maybe it was no more than coincidence. Weird. Even frightening. But no more than coincidence. Maybe.

'Dad.' Ben turned to his father as the Land Rover began the steep descent down Portlecombe Hill to the small town below.

'What?'

'Dad, she was really frightened.'

* * *

The wooden-framed kitchen clock hanging on the wall began to chime. Eight o'clock. As Lindsay looked out through the small cottage window and over the harbour, the light was already starting to fade and already many of the small boats, bobbing up and down on their moorings, lay in shadow. The tide was high.

Lindsay could hear her grandfather coughing in the room next door. At least he was still awake. More often than not, when he went to read his newspaper after supper, he fell asleep in the tall-backed chair that stood beside the window. She didn't like the coughing. Her grandfather hadn't seemed well recently.

She turned away from the window. Ben was late. She wondered if he had noticed anything in her voice when she'd phoned. Surprise. Worry. Fear perhaps. As she picked up the small yellow packet that had been lying on the table beside her, she remembered that she had felt all those emotions when she had first seen what had happened. And bewilderment.

In a world which, not long ago, had seemed no more than long, hot summer days spent in boats and at the water's edge, or even taking photographs for what now seemed an almost irrelevant school project, there was now the presence of darkness. As a child, she had been frightened by the thoughts of ghosts that move quietly in the night. Now, suddenly, she was a child again.

There was a knock on the door.

'Ben?'

'Sorry I'm late,' he said, walking into the narrow hallway. Lindsay nodded towards the kitchen.

'How's your gran?'

They sat at the kitchen table, Lindsay listening quietly as Ben told her of the nightmare. Of how his grandmother had quite suddenly sat up and screamed with fear at someone or something only she could see.

'It doesn't really make any sense,' said Ben thoughtfully, as he finished.

Lindsay waited for a moment and then leant forwards, pushing the small yellow packet across the table.

'Nor does this.'

Ben picked it up.

'Photographs?'

Lindsay nodded.

'The ones I took of the house.'

Puzzled, Ben opened the packet, taking the photographs out of it. They were upside down. He turned them over. The first was a wide-angled view of the ruins and the surrounding wasteland that had once been gardens. It might have been slightly out of focus but, other than that, there was nothing unusual. The second was a shot of some bricks, lying amongst tall grass. It didn't seem very interesting but Ben wasn't going to say anything. The third and fourth photographs were of what was left of the roof. He looked up.

'What am I looking for?'

'Keep going.'

There were three more at different angles of one side of the house and it wasn't until the ninth picture that Ben found it. He was suddenly very still, aware, for the first time, of the ticking of the clock on the wall.

'Is that for real?' said Lindsay.

Ben nodded.

'I think so.'

His voice was quiet. Strained.

* * *

Later that evening, long after Ben had gone home, and long after his granddaughter had kissed him goodnight and gone upstairs to bed, Tom Walker found the photographs on the mantlepiece, tucked behind one of the two heavy brass candlesticks. He took them down and, opening the packet, he slowly began to thumb through them. Outside, in the night, he heard the screech of a sea bird as it circled through the air. His hands were steady, his face calm. It was almost as if he knew what he was looking for.

At last, he found it. He nodded slowly and grunted softly to himself, almost as if to acknowledge that he'd been right all along.

The picture had been taken at the front of the house. The holes in its face where the windows had been. The gaping mouth that had once been the front doors. An empty, ruined house. Deserted, but for one person. Standing on the top of the wide stone steps that led to the doorway, there could clearly be seen the image of a small, red-haired girl. Smiling.

6

The small town hall had been built more or less in the centre of Portlecombe. Sitting on the edge of Fore Street, the single narrow road that curled its way through the centre of the town, the building proudly boasted the date of 1919, carved, for all to see, into a large rectangular slab of granite that sat above the wooden entrance doors.

The hall had been built to celebrate the homecoming of the town's heroes of the First World War. Those lucky few who had survived the horrors of the Western Front. The names of those who had not were etched into the granite beneath the date.

Twelve names. Fishermen who had known little of machine-guns. Or poison gas. Or war.

As he looked up at the names, Ben once again picked out the word 'Carson'. Private WG Carson. Killed in action. The Somme, 1916.

'What does that make him?' said Lindsay.

'History, I'm afraid,' said Ben.

'Your great grandfather?'

'Almost. He was my great grandfather's brother. William Gladstone Carson.' Ben turned to her and smiled. 'Wonderful name for a fisherman.'

'Is that what he was?'

'It's what they all were in those days.'

Standing in the morning sunshine, the street around them busy with holiday-makers bustling from shop to shop, laughing, chattering, smiling, neither Ben nor Lindsay could imagine the misery that lay behind each of those names. That not one of those young fishermen had reached the age of twenty. That not one of them had seen the man who killed him. That none of them had wanted to go.

'Ben.' Lindsay was looking up at the stone again. 'When was the Second World War?'

Ben looked at her. 'What is this? A history lesson?'

'No, it's just that . . . ' Lindsay squinted her eyes as she studied the stone above her, narrowing them against the harsh glare of the sun reflected from the windows of the building. 'Well, it didn't start in 1936, did it?'

'No. 1939. To be precise.'

'So what are those names then?'

Ben looked up at the stone. Beneath the details of those who had died in the trenches of northern France, there was written, in smaller letters, the date 1936. And then a list of seven names that ran from left to right across the face of the stone. Annie. Harry. John. William. Lizzie. Lol. And then, oddly, Laughing Boy.

Ben shrugged his shoulders. 'I don't know. They sound like children.'

Lindsay looked back to him. 'Haven't you ever asked anyone?'

'I once asked Gran.'

'And?'

There were sudden screams of laughter as two children ran in front of them, one throwing a ball high in the air before catching it again. And then they were gone, threading in and out of the shoppers in the street.

'And nothing. She said she didn't know.'

'And that's all?'

'That's all.'

Lindsay said nothing for a few moments. She wondered whether her own grandfather knew any more.

'Come on then. Or are we standing out here all day?'

Lindsay smiled. 'Sorry.'

She took him by the arm and they moved quickly through the sunshine towards the wooden doors.

Inside, the air was cooler. The thick stone walls of the town hall had been built — like those of the farmhouses in the surrounding Devon countryside — to keep the warmth in during the long cold winter evenings and to keep it out during the long hot summer days. Lindsay shivered slightly, her eyes slowly adjusting from the bright sunshine outside to the shadows of the hall.

'Where do we start?' she said, glancing at Ben.

'Wherever you like,' he said. 'It's your project.'

'Perhaps I can help.' Almost as if from nowhere, a tall man had appeared at a desk, some yards to their right. Ben had noticed the desk as they'd walked in. He hadn't seen the man.

'I, er . . . '

'It's me, really.' Lindsay had recovered quickly from the surprise of the man's sudden appearance. 'I've got a school project.'

'Project?'

The man was still standing behind the desk, leaning slightly forwards, as if having difficulty hearing what Lindsay was saying. Despite the lines of age about his face, there was yet a sparkle in his eyes that suggested an active mind. Presumably, he looked after the small museum.

' 'Images of Yesterday'. That's what it's called. I'm supposed to be taking photographs that might suggest how people used to live.'

The curator nodded slowly.

'I see.'

'We just thought Lindsay might get some ideas from here.'

Ben waved his arm towards the walls covered with photographs and the small wood-and-glass display cabinets that stood on the bare floor of the hall.

It had been many years since the town hall had played any useful role in Portlecombe's life. The days of local government had long gone and, after several years of falling into disuse, the building had eventually been given a new lease of life as a museum. A tribute to

Portlecombe and its past. 'No more'n a seaside junk shop', had been the view of one or two less charitable townspeople when it had first opened but, for Brian Talleyard, it had been an opportunity.

Although the Talleyard family name went far back into the history of Portlecombe, Talleyard himself had spent most of his life travelling abroad, his work as a mining engineer taking him from one continent to another for nearly thirty-five years. It had been a hard way of life and not one that he'd ever been genuinely committed to and, when the chance of an early retirement was offered, he had been only to happy to say goodbye and to retreat to the small cottage on the cliffs of Portlecombe that had belonged to his father. There, he was quite happy to live out the rest of his days to the sound of no more than the gulls crying overhead and the waves of the sea breaking against the rocks below him.

In the years that followed, he had begun to study his family's history. Perhaps because of the many years spent abroad, he felt that he was lacking any real identity. Perhaps he felt some deep-rooted need to find out who he was. And where he'd come from. He had also picked up his father's love of the countryside and he was never happier than when pulling strange-looking beetles from the depths of bushes or pinning brightly-coloured butterflies to his walls. He'd been pleased to agree to be curator of the museum when they'd asked him. He knew his father would have approved. Now he stood, watching Ben and Lindsay carefully as they explained that they didn't really know what they were looking for, except for ideas.

'Well,' he said, at last. 'Perhaps you'd better just wander around to begin with. Try and get a feel for the place. The oldest pictures are over there.' He pointed to the wall behind them. 'Most of them were taken more or less at the turn of the century. Those ones, there. And if you look along to the right, there's some from . . .'

As he spoke, his thick, wrinkled fingers began to trace a pattern along the smooth whitewashed walls. In almost the same way that wild flowers are crushed between the pages of a book or wild moths pinned to a board, the life and past of Portlecombe seemed now to have been framed and posted to the stone walls of a disused town hall, a building once dedicated to the memory of the dead.

The entrance doors opened again, slowly, the woman opening them almost as if treating them with reverence.

'Can I bring my dog in?'

Talleyard looked across at her and then back at Ben and Lindsay. 'Excuse me.'

Ben and Lindsay smiled and turned to move towards the photographs as Talleyard made his way to the door.

The earliest ones were very faded. Stern, unsmiling faces, indistinct and fading slowly into a blurred sepia wash, stared across the century. Their positions were staged. A family group with mother and father at the centre, the mother's head slightly stooped in deference to the proud, whiskered pose of her husband, both surrounded by a group of clumsily-dressed, sullen children. A fisherman in baggy trousers, tied at their bottoms with string, leaning nonchalantly against an upturned boat, a pipe in his mouth, netting in his hands. Three fishermen standing against a background of the harbour, their hands in their pockets, one wearing what looked like a battered bowler hat.

'Why don't they smile?' said Lindsay.

'I suppose they thought they had to take it seriously,' said Ben. 'After all, they probably didn't really even know what a camera was. Or what it did to them.'

'Like some tribes in South America.'

'What?'

'True,' said Lindsay. 'They think if you point a camera at them and take a picture, it robs them of their soul.'

Briefly, the image of the young girl standing at the open door flickered through her mind. She fought it. Buried it. That's why Ben had encouraged her to start her project again. To forget what had happened. Almost to pretend that it hadn't.

They moved slowly down the wall, the photographs becoming sharper, clearer as the years rolled by. Here, there were the returning heroes from the First World War. There, a ceremonial raising of the Union Jack beside the harbour front. Over here, what was perhaps the first car ever to visit Portlecombe. And down there, a blurred vision of the small fishing fleet lying at anchor in the harbour.

The recurring theme was the sea. And the land. The fishing boats. The cliffs. The harvests. The pale stoops of corn. Both fishermen and farmers alike had depended entirely on the natural world around them for their living. For their survival. It was hardly surprising therefore that the photographers of the time should have chosen to set their subjects against that background.

'Ben, look at this.'

'What?'

'Come here.'

Lindsay waved him across to a carefully mounted set of small wooden-framed photographs, each one featuring a group of school-children. They had been neatly set out in rows, each with a date written beneath it.

'What am I looking at?' said Ben, his eyes scanning the carefully posed groups.

'It's the local school,' said Lindsay. 'Look, it's every year through the twenties and thirties. Between the two wars. I suppose they must have closed the place when the second one began.'

'I suppose my grandad will be here somewhere,' said Ben, stooping slightly to look more closely at the pictures. 'And yours.'

Lindsay smiled. 'I don't think we'll recognize them.'

'Maybe not,' said Ben. 'But at least they look as if they're enjoying themselves.'

'Unlike the fishermen.'

Ben laughed.

Then he noticed a young boy standing at one end of a line. A broad grin spread from ear to ear and the sense of fun in his face seemed to burst from the picture itself. It was as if he was about to break into laughter and that no one in the world could fail to share the joke with him.

'I mean, look at this guy here, he's . . .'

'Ben.'

Lindsay's voice was still once more. The darkness had returned.

'Ben, that's Laughing Boy.'

'Who?'

'The names outside. That's Laughing Boy. I know it is.'

Ben thought of the granite. The names. The dates.

'But that was 1936. This picture was taken in 1935. Look, it says so.'

'Ben.' Lindsay was looking carefully at him now. 'Ben, you're not thinking. Laughing Boy was there in 1935. But then something happened to him in 1936. And to the other children. That's why their names are on the board.'

'Come on Linds,' said Ben, hoping the sudden dryness at the back of his throat wasn't affecting his voice. 'We don't even know if the names are children's.'

'No, but . . . '

'But nothing.'

Ben smiled, anxious to calm the fear he could see at the back of Lindsay's eyes. 'Look, old Laughing Boy's probably still smiling in 1936.'

'Ben.' Lindsay was shaking her head slowly, almost absently. 'There isn't a picture for 1936. It's missing.'

Ben carefully ran his eyes along the rows. From 1919 to 1939. Twenty years. There was a photograph of the village school for each of those years. Except for one.

'Excuse me . . . ' He turned quickly, his voice raised, looking for the curator.

But Talleyard had gone. The desk was empty. Their only company in the room was a woman and a small dog that she held on the end of a long lead.

* * *

The sea was flat.

Gazing out across it from the small

his forehead. He wiped it away with the cuff of his heavy overcoat.

'They built them solid in those days,' said Tom, surprised to find himself speaking in little more than a whisper.

Donald coughed, shivering slightly in a night-time wind that had grown colder.

'Better walk on,' he said. 'Best to get it over with.'

Tom nodded, murmuring his agreement. He turned the torch to his right and they began to follow what appeared to be the outline of a path running round the edges of what had once been a large, manicured lawn. Now, it was little more than a wasteland, presided over by the tall, spreading cedar tree that had thickened and stretched out its branches over the years.

The path was taking them closer to the sea. The salt from the spray on the rocks below them was carried on the wind and the sound of the breakers rolled up the cliff-face to meet them. They were now at some distance from the house. Ahead, whenever Tom raised the torch to peer into the distance, they could just see the outline of the rocky outcrop that stood on the edges of the cliff. It was overgrown now and as they neared it, they could make out the tangle of bushes that had sprung up at either side, almost as if in an attempt to disguise it.

'Is that it?' said Donald, quietly. His pulse had begun to quicken.

'That's it,' said Tom, holding the beam of the torch firmly on the mound in front of them.

They had begun to walk more slowly, almost as if afraid of their journey's end. The noise of the sea below blocked out all other sounds, its interminable rhythms seemingly creating a barrier between the two men and the world they had left behind them.

As they reached the mound, they stopped.

It was taller than the two men and stretched away at either side of them until its edges sloped down to the ground. It might as easily have been a large rock, laid there, on the edges of the cliffs, many thousands of years before by the fabled giants of the Devon coastline. Or a Stone Age burial mound, where the ghosts of the long-dead might spend eternity gazing out to sea. It was neither. It was no more than a freak of nature, an outcrop thrown up when first the cliffs had squeezed together and settled into place. Once it had been much taller and had no doubt stood proudly as a beacon to the seas beyond. Weathered by many centuries, it had now been laid low, so low that it seemed vulnerable to the claws of the brambles and tangleweed that overran it.

Glancing past it and far out across the sea beyond, Tom could see the distant, pulsing light of the Eddystone lighthouse. For a moment, quite suddenly, he thought of the cold November evening when that light had saved his life.

'Are we going in?'

Donald's voice broke into his thoughts, dragging him equally suddenly back into the present. A dark, pitiless night on the edges of the Portlecombe cliffs.

'It's what we've come here for,' he said quickly and handed Donald the torch.

With his walking stick, he now began to beat back the tangle of bushes that had grown across the rock. Sometimes levering them, sometimes simply battering them into submission, he slowly cleared them away, revealing finally what lay behind.

In the light of the torch, they could both see the slanting crack that ran across the face of the stone.

'Still here then,' said Donald.

'Didn't expect it to disappear, did you?' said Tom, almost surprised.

'No, it's just that . . .'

'I know,' said Tom. 'When you've never seen something. Only heard about it.'

'Just didn't know what to expect, I suppose.'

They stood for a moment, looking at the crack. A crack broad enough for one man to pass through, a crack that marked the entrance to the labyrinth of caves that ran deep below. At either side of it, the broken stumps of the brambles shifted slightly in the wind, scratching the rock.

'I'll go first,' said Donald.

He stepped forwards, the torchlight now threading through the crack. He turned his body side-on to the rock and slowly squeezed himself through the opening. As he disappeared inside, so Tom now followed him, surprised to find that the crack was wider than it seemed. Moments later, both were through the entrance and now facing the steep shale descent to the caves below.

Neither man had noticed the small

shadowed figure that had been watching them from the edges of the gardens.

* * *

At first, Donald found it difficult to keep his footing. The stone sides of what seemed to be a corridor were smooth and offered few handholds. The ground beneath his feet was loose stone which slid away all too easily. He had fallen once, dropping the torch. Fortunately, it had not broken.

Tom followed him, bowing his head. It wasn't the fear of hitting it against the stone — the rocky ceiling was high above his head — it was simply that, winding his way deeper and deeper into the cliff, following what Nature had created thousands of years ago as a natural tunnel, he felt frightened, cowed. He had never liked confined spaces which was why he now drew in upon himself, almost as if in protection against some unknown horror.

Neither of them knew how long it took to reach the bottom. It might have been five minutes. Or fifty-five.

The path had been much as they had been told. Winding, narrow, hot. Both had worried about the torch. Deep in the cliff, there would have been no natural light. Just the primeval darkness that had been there since time began. And with the darkness, the fear that they were at the mercy of forces that they barely dared to contemplate. The light, at least, seemed to keep those fears at bay. At last, the narrow corridor seemed to widen. The slippery gravel seemed to give way to a more permanent, harder floor and the slope lessened until it was almost flat.

'Sssh!'

Donald turned to Tom behind him.

'Listen.'

The two men stood silently, their bodies taut, their hearts pumping. Ahead, they could hear a steady drip. The sound of small drops of water falling into what might be a pool. A sound enhanced by the echo of a cave.

'This must be it,' whispered Tom.

Slowly, they edged forwards, the corridor wall turning gently to the left. As they moved forwards, so the drip grew louder. They could smell the salt water. They had to be at sea level. The ground was now flat.

And then, quite suddenly, the final

corner turned, they found themselves standing at the edges of a cave. Here the torchlight scanned the tall rounded sides of the chamber, the hard stone platform before them, the dark waters of a pool beyond. It was exactly what they had been told they would find.

And still the water dripped.

'I don't believe it,' muttered Tom.

'How did they ever know about this place?' said Donald, his eyes searching the furthest crannies of the cave that the torch could reach.

'One of them found it by chance. The story goes that, back in those days, it was the village idiot who stumbled across it while he was out looking for mermaids.'

The two men were silent again. Slowly, Donald moved the beam of the torch toward the centre of the chamber. Both knew what must be there. Neither wanted to see.

The stone box was still on the floor. Beside it, lying on its side, its glass panes shattered, was a lantern. The lid of the box had been moved and was now propped against its side. Donald looked across at Tom.

'I know. It's what we've come here for.'

Tom nodded, unsmiling.

Keeping the box in the light of the torch, they walked slowly towards it. As they approached, their gaze was fixed on what might be inside. The sound of their shoes tapping on the hard stone floor echoed, each wave growing fainter only to be replaced by another as each step took the men nearer to the opened stone box.

They reached it. Tom stopped. Donald walked on, circling the box until he stood with his back to the dark pool beyond. They said nothing.

The stone box was empty.

'Then it is her,' said Tom, at last.

Deep in a corner of the cave, the water continued to drip.

Donald looked across at his friend.

'I'm afraid so.'

Tom shook his head slowly.

'Then may God help us all.'

Neither of them could have known about the creature. Nor even seen it as it screwed its way up through the black waters of the pool only to burst through the surface like a bloodied hand bursting through a pane of glass.

It seemed to Tom as he first caught sight of it that the water had boiled, erupted in a towering spume of white water, and thrown up a creature from the furthest depths of Hell. A dark, blurred, writhing shape amidst the cascading, churning brine that now hung above them, its eyes glittering behind the line of its teeth.

'Donald!'

Instinctively, Tom reached across the box, grabbing Donald by the lapels of his coat. Terrified, Donald had looked up to see the creature rearing above him, its black eyes fixed on him, its jaws opening as it now began to fall.

He screamed. An ear-piercing scream that howled around the cave as the creature fell on him. Tom, still clinging to Donald's coat, stretched across the stone box, found himself eye to eye with the monster as it closed its jaws around the old man and began to fall back into the water, pulling him across the floor. Helplessly, Tom watched as his friend was dragged from his grasp and pulled down into the black, boiling waters of the pool.

'Donald!'

And then, quite suddenly, all was quiet again. The echoes died, the waters calmed, the drip returned.

Tom lay quite still for some moments. What had happened, he had seen. But he didn't believe it. It was all no more than a terrifying dream and soon he would wake up. As he lay on the cold stone floor, he was a child once again, a child lying awake in the depths of night listening to the scratch of a tree branch on the window and thinking that Satan himself had come to find him.

'Tom.'

He heard the voice. He heard the gentle splashing of water. It was no more than part of the dream. A change of direction. A turn of the head on the pillow.

'Tom. Help.'

The voice was soft, frightened. Desperate. Once more the water was splashing.

At last, Tom turned his head. Reaching for the torch which was still lying where Donald had dropped it, he turned it slowly towards the sound of the voice. Floating on the surface of the pool, feebly splashing with his arms as if trying to reach the side, Donald was calling to his friend.

'Tom. Help, please.'

Struggling to his feet, his heart suddenly pounding, Tom saw the walking stick lying by the stone box. He grabbed it, held it over the water's surface, within Donald's reach.

'Grab it, Donald! Quick! Before that thing comes back!'

He was shouting. Almost hysterically.

Feebly, Donald's hands closed around the stick. Tom pulled at the other end, moving Donald closer and closer to the edge of the pool.

'Help, Tom. Please.'

Donald was murmuring, almost to himself.

As he reached the side of the pool, Tom reached down and pulled his friend out of the water. He was cold. His clothes were torn. There was an ugly gash on his right leg. But, incredibly, he was alive.

'I don't know how,' said Tom after a few minutes. 'I really don't know how, but I'll get you out of here.'

* * *

The dawn was breaking in the eastern skies when the two men finally crawled through the crack in the cliff-top rock.

Somehow, crawling, limping, carrying, Tom Walker had managed to help Donald back to the top of the stone tunnel and now, exhausted, they both stood and gazed out over a lead grey sea that they thought never to have seen again. Still some distance from the top, their torch had finally gone out and the last hour of their climb had been in darkness.

'Tom.'

Donald's voice was weak. Barely audible.

'Don't talk,' said Tom.

'I . . . I just want to say . . . '

'Don't talk, Donald. Just take it easy.'

'Why shouldn't he talk? He just wanted to say thank you.'

The voice was high-pitched. The voice of a child.

Tom Walker stiffened. He turned slowly, his right hand tightening on the stick he still carried. There, in the cold, grey light of dawn, some three metres from them, stood the girl. Smiling.

'Now will you come to my party?'

'Witch!'

Tom howled, and lifting his stick furiously, high above his head, he brought it crashing down on her. It hit the ground, splintering on the rocks that lay just beneath the surface of the cliff-top heather.

The girl had gone.

Falling to his knees, Tom finally wept, his head cupped in his hands, his shoulders heaving up and down. Donald, slowly, painfully, knelt beside him, putting an arm across his back.

'Don't worry, Tom. We'll find a way.'

And in the east, the sun had begun to rise.

8

‘So they were right, then.’

‘Who?’

Donald swirled the dark brown whisky round in his glass. He looked across the fireside at Tom.

‘All those years ago, the fishermen used to talk about the Portlecombe eel. Everyone knew it was there. No one had ever seen it.’

Tom nodded. He knew the stories too.

They’d started at the turn of the century when a fishing boat had capsized just outside the harbour. A rescue boat was launched but by the time they’d been able to row out to the stricken vessel, the four crewmen had disappeared. Over the next few days, they’d searched for any evidence of what might have happened to the men but without success, and it wasn’t until a farm worker came forward that any clue emerged.

The man said he’d been cutting corn in the fields above the cliffs on the afternoon the boat had turned over. The weather hadn't been good and when it had started to rain, he'd decided to call it a day and go home. It had been whilst he was walking home along those cliffs that he'd seen the boat in trouble. It was obviously struggling against the heavy seas and when it was finally hit by a savage gust of wind, it had simply keeled over, throwing its crew into the water. At first, they'd started swimming for the shore. The man said he'd been able to see them quite clearly.

According to the story, before he went on to say what happened next, the man had asked for a bible and when he was given one, he had taken it in his hand and sworn that what he was about to say was the truth.

As the men had swum through the water, an enormous black snake had emerged from the waves, towering above them, then falling on each one in turn. It had picked up each of the fishermen in its mouth, shaken them from side to side and then disappeared once again beneath the water. Despite the distance, the man said he had still been able to hear their screams, a sound he would take to his grave.

Tom remembered his father telling him the story.

They'd been out fishing and he smiled as he thought of how he'd spent the rest of the afternoon peering anxiously over the side of the boat into the depths below, just in case there might be a long black shadow following them. And now, after all this time, he had finally seen the shadow.

'What I don't understand,' said Donald, gazing once again into the small fire, 'is why the thing let me go.'

Outside, darkness had at last begun to fall on the long summer evening.

'It's her,' said Tom.

'Who?'

'The girl.' He sipped his whisky. 'She controls them. Plays with them. Just like she's playing with us.'

He leant forwards and picking another log from the small hearthside basket, threw it on to the fire.

'Your leg still hurting?'

'I've known worse,' said Donald. He rubbed it slowly just above the knee, where the eel had fastened its mouth. 'What are we going to do?'

'I don't know,' said Tom. 'Maybe . . .' His voice trailed off.

'Maybe what?'

'Well, maybe . . . maybe she'll just go away again.'

The small front door of the cottage opened, briefly letting in the sounds of the street outside before closing again.

'Hello, Grandad.'

Lindsay's voice sounded happy. It was enough to break through the traces of fear that had begun to surround the two old men.

'We're in here, Lindsay.'

Lindsay's face appeared round the living-room door. She smiled when she saw them.

'Well, well. Having a night in, are we?'

* * *

Later, when Donald had long gone and as they sat stirring cups of hot chocolate in the kitchen, Lindsay looked across the table at her grandfather, at his tired, reddened eyes.

'You need to go to bed,' she said.

'Yes. I know.'

'Grandad.'

'Yes?'

'Where were you last night?'

The old man looked up. He couldn't lie to his granddaughter. But neither could he tell her the truth. 'I'm afraid I can't tell you, Lindsay.'

'Why not?'

'It wasn't important.'

'Well, if it wasn't important . . . ' She stopped. And then smiled. Everyone needs to have a secret.

* * *

Ben was waiting outside the town hall. Further up the town, St Peter's church clock was chiming. Ten o'clock. The hall should be opening.

'Hi.'

'Is he here?'

Lindsay was breathless, having run from her grandfather's cottage.

'Haven't looked,' said Ben.

'Come on.'

They tried the wooden doors. They were locked. Peering in through one of the windows to the side, Ben couldn't see any sign of life.

'Maybe it's shut today.'

'In the holidays?' said Lindsay. 'It's the only time they can make any money.'

‘OK, so we’re early.’

Lindsay smiled. ‘Well, at least it’s not raining.’

It was almost ten minutes before Mrs Dodds arrived. A tall, elegant woman, wearing a long, multi-coloured chiffon scarf that seemed to billow out behind her like a sail as she cut her way through the shoppers bustling in the small street.

‘Good morning,’ she said, arriving finally at the town hall doors. ‘I’m sorry if I’m late. Don’t tell old Talleyard whatever you do. He’d have a fit. Anyway, I can’t remember when we last had a queue.’

As she spoke, she fiddled furiously in a large leather handbag.

‘Don’t worry. I know I’ve got them here somewhere, I always put them in here so the dog can’t get them. Must be the only dog in the entire county with an obsession for keys. Ah.’ She pulled out a large, single key. ‘In we go.’

Plunging the key into the keyhole, she wound it viciously round, pushing the doors with her shoulders at the same time. The doors opened. ‘Come in, come in.’

Ben and Lindsay followed her inside, watching as she flicked the light switches and thumbed quickly through the mail before dropping it on the desk.

She turned to them. 'Now, how can I help?'

'We were looking for the curator,' said Ben.

'You've found her.'

'No . . . I meant . . . '

'We were looking for the other one,' said Lindsay. 'The gentleman.'

'Ah, old Talley, you mean,' beamed Mrs Dodds. 'Well, you won't find him here today. It's his day off.'

'Well, it's just that . . .'

'Perhaps I can help.'

'It's about the photographs,' said Ben.

'Then I can't help. The only person who knows anything at all about them is old Talley. Personally, I think they all look as deadly as sin.'

Mrs Dodds smiled broadly.

'Do you know — ?' Ben began.

'Do I know where he is? No, but if you really want me to have a guess, he'll be fishing filthy things out of the ponds in Gerston Valley. It's his hobby, you know. Natural history. Can't say I'm very interested.'

* * *

'Dytiscus larvae. One of the most revolting things you'll ever come across.'

Talleyard knelt beside the pond and pulled out a thick, black glistening creature in his tweezers. It twitched in the sunlight. 'Do you know what it does?'

Ben and Lindsay shook their heads, wondering for a moment if it had really been a good idea to go looking for the curator.

'I'll tell you. It's got four jaws at the front here, and when it sees a tasty bit of lunch swimming along, a tadpole, a stickleback, water lice or whatever, it clamps all four of them on to the luckless creature and then squirts an enzyme into the wound. That turns whatever it is into liquid and then old Dytiscus here simply sucks it up like soup. Charming.'

Neither Lindsay nor Ben wanted to ask what an enzyme might be.

'And it's no better when it grows up either. The Dytiscus beetle is one of the most bad-tempered creatures in the English countryside.'

Talleyard dropped the creature back into the pond.

'Curious, don't you think? A beautiful day, a beautiful country pond. And things like that crawling around just below the surface.'

The ponds stood at the head of the Gerston valley, some miles north of the town. There were three of them, fed by a small stream that finally wound down the valley to meet the sea at the edges of a small beach. On one side of them, wild, tangled brambles gave way finally to a small wood, whilst on the other stood the tall, golden stalks of a barley field, waiting for the harvester.

Talleyard was sitting beside the largest of the three ponds. At his side were his various collecting jars and boxes. He had now picked up his fishing-rod again and was preparing to cast the line out over the water.

'Not that there's many around,' he said, as he brought the rod back and then flicked it forwards, the thin gut-line snaking through the air before settling on to the water.

'What are you fishing for?' said Ben.

'Carp.'

'Carp?' said Lindsay.

Talleyard gazed out over the pond impassively.

'It's quite a common fish. Silvery,

golden scales. Can be quite big.' He turned and looked at her. 'They don't normally take your hand off.'

He nodded towards the wicker basket. 'There's some sandwiches in there.'

The midday sun was warm. Talleyard took off his straw Panama hat, wiping the back of his hand across his forehead.

'You didn't come all the way up here to ask me about carp, did you?'

Ben shook his head. 'We were wondering about the photographs.'

'Ah yes,' said Talleyard. 'The project.'

'No, not the project,' said Lindsay. 'Not any more.'

There was a slight pull on the line. Talleyard felt it. The fish was nudging the bait. Testing it.

'If it's not the project . . . ?' He let the question hang in the air. The fish had come back, this time more strongly.

'What happened in 1936?'

As the fish attacked the bait, dangling inches above the muddy bottom of the pool, so Talleyard struck, wrenching the line backwards, catching the hook in the side of the fish's mouth. He began to wind the line in, hard.

'There are twenty years of school

photographs in the museum,' said Lindsay. 'Except for one. 1936. It's missing.'

Viciously, Talleyard span the reel.

'We never had it,' he grunted. 'Got lost somewhere.'

The tightened line now edged closer to the bank as the fish zig-zagged its way towards them, held in place by the line.

'What about the children's names?' said Ben.

'What children?'

'On the front of the building. Underneath the names from the First World War.'

They could see the fish, swimming just below the surface, having given up the fight and now simply floating, half on its back, as Talleyard pulled it into the bank.

'The names? They weren't children.'

'Who were they?'

Talleyard lifted the fish out of the water with a small net and, putting his hand to its mouth, he began to work the hook loose.

'Daytrippers, I'm afraid. Down for a day's pleasure boating. Hired a boat. Sea got rough. The boat sank. They drowned.'

'So why are they all children's names?'

'Those were the names they gave to the boat's owner.'

The hook was embedded. Talleyard had to tear it loose.

'He should never have hired it to them, of course. They obviously didn't know what they were doing.'

'And that was in 1936?'

'Yes.'

Talleyard smiled briefly and, opening the wicker basket, he dropped the dying fish inside it. Both Ben and Lindsay knew he was lying but didn't know why.

Ben glanced at his watch.

'I'm afraid I hadn't realized how late it was. I'm supposed to be meeting Dan on the quay at half past.'

'Dan?'

'My brother.'

* * *

Talleyard watched as they walked slowly away down the valley toward the beach. They would turn left and take the winding coastal road into town. Half an hour, perhaps. At one point, they turned and waved. Talleyard nodded. And then turned back to the pond. A slight breeze was now throwing ripples across the surface.

Standing by the edges of the water, he swung the tall rod back over his shoulder again, waited for a moment and then threw it forwards, letting the line run out from the reel. He was looking for the deeper water where he knew the carp would be feeding.

The line fell short.

He moved to his left. The long, sweeping branches of the willow tree that stood at the head of the pond were now closer to him.

He wound the line back in. Carefully, he brought the rod back again, then swung it forwards, flinging the twisting line high into the air, out towards the centre of the pool. He watched as it traced an arc through the air, and then grunted as it now fell towards the willow branches, drifting in what might have been a light gust of wind.

Talleyard dropped the rod. He walked slowly round the edges of the water, wondering whether to simply tear the line down or perhaps climb up and free it. The branch looked strong enough. And low enough for him to be able to climb up to it.

He decided that he would try to free it.

The trunk of the willow offered a series of convenient handholds for him to be able to pull himself up. One foot on a distended whorl on the side of the tree, the other on the stump of a broken branch, he began to climb. It was easier than he thought it would be. He reached the branch that spread out over the pool. It would be foolish to crawl along it but he could see that, if he held the branches above and then shuffled along the actual branch, he could then jump gently up and down on it and so shake the line loose.

Carefully, he eased himself into position, his hands above his head, his feet now edging slowly out above the water. He felt slightly irritated that he'd forgotten to take his hat off.

The lower branch swayed slightly. He stopped, sweat now breaking out on his forehead. It had been a foolish decision. It wouldn't have been expensive to replace the line.

The branch stopped swaying. He began to move forwards again. And it was then that he looked down.

The girl was floating just beneath the surface of the water. Her head was looking up towards him, her eyes black, her lips slightly parted. Slowly, she smiled, her mouth widening, her long red hair drifting out into the eddies of the pool.

* * *

At the bottom of the valley, Lindsay and Ben heard the scream, so faint that it might have been a bird.

They looked quickly at each other. And then began to run. The valley was steep, the uneven ground was thick with grass. The muscles of their legs began to ache and then to sear with pain, but yet they ran. They reached the third pond. Then the second.

'Ben!'

Lindsay screamed and pointed. Floating on the surface of the pond was the straw hat.

Running to the water's edge, Ben hurled himself into the water and struck out across the surface. He reached the hat. He looked down into the pool. Talleyard's body was lying on the bottom, almost as if held down by the weeds. Ben plunged under the water, reaching out, grabbing the man by the shoulders, dragging him to the surface. Painfully, he began to stagger backwards, the water just shallow enough for him to touch the bottom with his feet. He could feel the pull of the weeds at his legs. The image of the beetle larvae flickered at the back of his mind.

And then he had reached the bank. Lindsay clambered down into the water. Together, they managed to roll Talleyard's body out of the pond and on to the grass. Ben pulled himself out and, turning Talleyard over so that he lay on his front, he began to push down on his back, a rhythmic, pumping action, forcing the lungs to work, forcing the vile pond water out of them. He knew that if he had got to him soon enough, this would work.

'Ben, he's . . .'

Talleyard had started coughing. Violent, shaking coughs that seemed to convulse his whole body and being. But the coughing brought the water out of his system. They had been in time. Ben rolled him on to his back, loosening his shirt buttons, giving him room to breathe.

It was then that Lindsay screamed.

As Ben drew the shirt back, so they could both see that Talleyard's chest was covered with glistening black larvae, each with its four jaws locked into his skin.

* * *

'I don't know,' said Lindsay. 'All we heard was a scream.'

'He was lucky.'

Her grandfather lit his pipe and looked out over the harbour from the small cottage garden.

'Lucky?'

'That you heard him.'

He blew small clouds of smoke into the warm air of the early evening.

'Will he be all right?'

'They said so when the ambulance turned up. It just looked so . . . horrible, I suppose.'

'I'm sure it did.'

They were silent for a few moments, listening to the call of the gulls and the gentle purr of a motor launch crossing the harbour.

'Grandad.'

Lindsay spoke without looking at him.

'Did you ever go on any pleasure trips when you were young? You know, trips around the bay. That sort of thing.'

The old man chuckled.

'Weren't no pleasure trips in Portle-combe in those days. The only boats that moved were fishing boats. Pleasure trips?' He chuckled again. 'I can't imagine what my dad would have said.'

'No,' said Lindsay. 'Nor can I.'

And as Tom Walker then drew on his pipe, he realized what he had said. The story of the pleasure trip had been what they'd all agreed.

9

It was mid-afternoon by the time Lindsay and Ben came in sight of the cottage.

It stood halfway down the cliffs overlooking the harbour entrance. Built originally as a coastguard's cottage, it had no longer served any useful purpose after the last coastguard left shortly after the turn of the century, and by 1916, when Talleyard's grandfather William bought it, it had fallen into considerable disrepair.

William was to spend the next two years rebuilding it, making a home fit for not only his wife and youngest son, Nathan, but most especially for his eldest son, Jack, who was fighting in the trenches of northern France.

Jack, the returning hero, never came home. He was shot through the head in France, three days before the end of the war.

William never recovered. For weeks after the news, he would walk along the lonely cliffs staring out to sea, his hands clasped behind his back, his face pitted against whatever weather was blowing in from the west.

And then, one day, he simply jumped.

They found his body spreadeagled across the rocks below, broken, like his heart and his mind. He was buried in the graveyard of St Peter's, a simple stone marking the life of a simple man. Jack's body never came back from France but his name joined the others on the town hall wall.

As Ben and Lindsay began to descend the steep, rock-face path that led from the top of the cliffs down to the cottage, they passed the outcrop of rock against which William had finally leant before leaping into space and tumbling two hundred feet through the air on to the black granite teeth below. He had screamed and for many years afterwards, his widow had sworn that she could still hear that scream, late at night, when the owls shriek.

'Do you think he's there?' said Lindsay, as she moved slowly down the narrow path, keeping her body tucked into the cliff face.

She didn't look to her left, where the cliff dropped down to the sea below. A rope dangled limply between a series of wooden posts that ran down the side of the path but it was unlikely to provide any comfort for those unlucky enough to slip and fall. Lindsay doubted if Talleyard had many visitors.

'There's smoke coming from the chimney,' said Ben. 'Look.'

He pointed to the small brick chimney that sat at the edge of the slate roof. A thin curl of blue smoke was drifting up into the air from it.

Lindsay smiled. 'Well, at least we haven't come all this way for nothing.'

As they neared the cottage, the path now became a series of stone steps, cut into the side of the cliff. It had taken William three months to carve them out but he had done his job well. They had weathered the test of time.

The cottage was painted white. Around the base of the walls, the whitewash was muddied, the result of rain splashing into the ground around it. The windows were small cold eyes, squinting out across the cold, grey, heaving wasteland of the sea beyond.

They stood outside the small front door. High above, a cormorant began to call, its thin voice looping through the dull skies. Rain had been forecast before the close of the day.

Ben knocked, rapping his knuckles against the hard wooden door.

There was no reply. No sound but for the cormorant above and the swell of the sea below. He knocked again.

'Mr Talleyard?' He called softly at first. And then more loudly. 'Mr Talleyard? It's only us. Ben and Lindsay.'

The cottage was still silent.

Ben reached for the smooth, rounded door handle. He turned it.

'Ben, I . . .'

'Linds, we're not about to burgle the place.'

The door opened. Slowly, Ben pushed it wider, looking past it into the gloom of the small room beyond. He stepped inside.

'Mr Talleyard?'

Lindsay followed him. They stood alone on the stone floor of the small kitchen. Somewhere, they could hear a clock ticking. They could no longer hear the sea, the thick cottage walls now blocked out the sound. The air was heavy with the scent of burning wood.

'Well, he must be around somewhere,' said Ben, softly. 'That fire next door didn't light itself.'

'Maybe he's asleep,' said Lindsay.

'Maybe.'

There was a movement in the corner of the room. With a howl, a small black creature suddenly hurled itself across the floor, brushing against Lindsay's leg. She gasped, falling backwards against the wooden kitchen table.

'Ben!'

Ben watched the cat disappear through the open front door. He smiled. And then noticed that his heart was suddenly beating hard too. He walked to the door leading into the next room and, opening it, went through.

This was clearly where Talleyard spent most of his time. A large, thickly-padded armchair sat beside the open fire. A circular piece of carpet lay on the floor in the centre of the room and at one side stood a wooden cabinet. It was open, its doors bent back to reveal a collection of glasses and a single, dark-coloured bottle. The glow of the fire brought a warmth to the room and the smoke, which from time to time blew from it, seemed to have softened it around the edges.

'It's like being back in the museum,' said Lindsay, as she stood in the doorway, her gaze travelling slowly round the room.

The fire crackled briefly.

Each wall was almost entirely covered with pictures. Unlike the bare, white surrounds of the kitchen, here the room was almost alive with images drawn from a vast catalogue of years gone by.

Huge black and white sailing ships charted their way across the walls. Small, precious cameos of elegantly styled young women crouched in the corners. Groups of bewhiskered farm workers stood glaring at the visitors, their arms folded over their chests, their backs leaning against a cart. There was no pattern to the display. It was almost as if the photographs and their frames had been nailed to the walls at random, a kaleidoscopic porridge of history, there for the observer to sift through and to select.

Drawn into the room, Ben and Lindsay began to make their way round it, staring, fascinated, at the pictures. They moved slowly, their eyes flickering over the memories of an age that now seemed golden but which had been, in reality, harsh and unforgiving.

It was as they neared the windows that Lindsay stopped, her attention caught by a small, wooden-framed picture.

'Ben.'

Ben turned.

'Look.'

A small group of school children were now staring at them from the wall. Almost exactly as they had been in the museum. The familiar chill had returned. Neither of them spoke. Beneath the picture, neatly handwritten on a small slip of paper, was a date. July, 1936. And standing near the centre of the group, smiling, was the girl.

'I might have known you'd come snooping.'

They both turned quickly. Neither had heard him come into the house, neither of them knew how long he had been there, standing in the doorway of the room, watching them.

'Mr Talleyard, we . . . '

Ben started to stammer an apology but then stopped as his gaze fell to Talleyard's right hand. It hung limply at his side, its fingers curled around the handle of a long, glittering knife.

* * *

The rain had now begun to fall. The skies had darkened and, as she closed the windows of the small hospital room, the nurse wondered if she shouldn't also be closing the curtains.

'What do you think?'

'Oh, I should leave them,' said Phoebe, leaning forward slightly in her bed. 'I've always quite enjoyed watching the rain.'

The nurse smiled.

'If that's what you'd like.'

She moved away from the window, folding a towel and then putting it on a rail at the foot of Phoebe's bed.

'How much longer?' Phoebe's voice sounded tired. Almost plaintive.

'I'm sorry?'

'How much longer do I have to stay here?'

The nurse finished arranging the towel and then stood back.

'Not too much longer, I'm sure.'

'But the doctor said I was looking better this morning. 'Soon have you out of here, Mrs Stone.' That's what he said.'

'And I'm sure he's right, Phoebe,' said the nurse, kindly.

She knew that the doctors were actually worried about the old woman. That her heart was very weak. That another attack would almost certainly be fatal. But there seemed little point in telling her that. The nurse moved towards the door. Then she turned.

'Oh, I almost forgot. Your granddaughter left you some flowers earlier this afternoon.'

'Granddaughter?'

'Yes. Sweet little thing. She turned up at reception with this enormous bunch of wild flowers that she said she'd picked herself. I'll ask one of the porters to bring them along. And I'll get him to bring a vase as well so we can put them on the window-sill.'

She smiled again, then left, letting the door close behind her.

Phoebe stared at the door and let her eyes cross the room until she found herself watching the patterns made by the falling rain against the glass panes of the window.

'But I haven't got a granddaughter,' she whispered.

* * *

Talleyard walked slowly across the room. Above them, they could hear the rain now drumming on the slate tiles. Neither Ben nor Lindsay moved. They watched carefully as Talleyard came towards them.

He stopped.

'Might have known,' he said quietly, slowly. 'Might have known you'd be back. Snooping.'

Ben was breathing fast. On a bookshelf to his right, there was what looked like a brass candlestick. He could probably reach it quickly enough.

Talleyard had stopped in the centre of the room. He stared at them. 'I couldn't find her, you know.'

Lindsay broke the silence. 'Who?'

'I would have killed her.'

'Who couldn't you find?'

His cold eyes turned towards Lindsay, studying her, much as the black mamba rears its head and watches the mouse with curiosity before lunging forwards to sink its fangs into the shivering creature.

'I would have killed her.'

He turned and moved slowly towards the large armchair. He lowered himself gently into it, letting the knife fall from his hand and clatter on to the stone floor. And then he sat without moving, his legs stretched out before him, gazing into the fire.

He now had his back to Lindsay and Ben, almost as if suddenly unaware of their presence. They waited for some minutes, listening to the clock ticking in the background, to the rain falling outside and to the logs crackling occasionally on the fire. Talleyard had begun to breathe deeply. When, at last, he began to snore, Ben looked across at Lindsay. She nodded. Quietly, they began to move towards the open door. But not before Ben had reached across to the wall and gently taken the photograph of the children off its hook.

⋆ ⋆ ⋆

'Is this it?'

The porter had picked up a large bunch of flowers, their stems wrapped tightly in heavy brown paper and tied with string.

The receptionist nodded. 'Room forty-eight. Mrs Stone.'

'Smell a bit, don't they?'

The receptionist looked up from her desk. 'They're wild.'

'Does that make any difference?'

'Evidently, it does.'

Hilary had little time for the hospital porters who, as far as she was concerned, were lazy and generally incompetent. She looked back to her computer screen.

Harry shrugged his shoulders and turned away, taking the flowers. He could have told her that he'd spent his morning-off playing chess with a child dying of leukemia. But he didn't. He walked on down the corridor, whistling quietly to himself. And, anyway, he was right. The flowers did smell.

Phoebe's room was on the second floor. Harry hadn't actually been to see her since she'd been in the hospital but he remembered the stories he'd heard. Something about a mad dog. He knocked on the door. At first, there was no reply. He knocked again.

'Come in.'

The voice was faint. Harry also now remembered that Mrs Stone was very ill. He pushed the door open with his foot and eased himself through it, carrying the flowers in front of him.

'Mrs Stone?'

Phoebe had been crying and her eyes were now red as she turned her head towards the door to look at her visitor.

Harry smiled. 'They're for you.'

Phoebe said nothing.

'From your granddaughter. She dropped them off.'

Phoebe struggled to move her lips. Her headache had returned. She spoke quietly.

'I don't have a granddaughter.'

A look of surprise briefly crossed Harry's face and then, as he moved towards her bed, he shook his head.

'Don't worry, Mrs Stone. They'll have got it wrong downstairs. That girl Hilary's got the brains of a plank.'

He laid the flowers on her bed. 'Anyway, you get yourself sitting up and have a look at these and I'll go off and find us a vase and some water.'

He leant forward and loosened the string that had held the flowers and turned and disappeared through the door, promising to be back soon.

Phoebe moved slightly against the pillows, making herself more comfortable. The porter's voice had been kindly. And maybe he was right. Maybe they had got it wrong downstairs. It could even have been Lindsay who had left the flowers.

Now she looked at them. Some of them

she recognized, others were new to her. They were wild, and whoever had chosen them had chosen them for their colour. Their heads were a wonderful profusion of bright, almost gaudy, reds, yellows and blues that now seemed to bring the room to life. She smiled as she looked at them.

And then her face stiffened. Suddenly breathing hard, she felt the pains coming back into her chest. By the window, something had moved.

* * *

Harry had found a vase in a washroom at the end of the corridor. It wasn't especially attractive but it would do. He had turned on the taps and begun to fill it when he heard the scream.

He turned sharply, dropping the vase into the enamel basin. It splintered.

Throwing himself at the narrow swing-doors of the washroom, Harry burst out into the corridor and ran down it. He had no doubt at all where the scream had come from. A doctor in a long white coat had appeared at the other end.

'Quick!' shouted Harry. 'Forty eight!'

He caught the door handle violently and swung the door open.

Phoebe was lying on the floor, quite still. Her bedclothes were scattered, torn from their neat folds on the bed as the old woman's body had fallen, dragging them with her. The flowers lay in a jumbled pile beside them.

Instinctively, Harry dropped to his knees, looking for life in the old woman, moving his hands under her back in an attempt to lift her into a sitting position.

'She alive?' The doctor had appeared at the doorway.

Harry didn't reply.

'Harry! Is she alive?'

Slowly, Harry eased Phoebe's body back on to the floor and moved back.

'What's that?' he whispered, his eyes now staring at the window.

The doctor turned.

'For pity's sake, Harry, I just — ' The words caught in his throat.

Outside, the rain was stopping, although neither man noticed. Both had seen the girl's face at the window. Smiling.

* * *

The museum was still open.

Mrs Dodds had thought of closing when the rain had started but then, she had reasoned, more people were likely to visit, even if only to shelter from the weather. She had been wrong. No more than five people had walked through the doors all afternoon and she'd been putting her coat on when Lindsay and Ben made it six and seven.

'I was almost closing,' she said as they appeared at the doors.

'We won't be a minute. Promise,' said Lindsay.

'We just want to check a photograph.'

'Five minutes?'

'Fine,' said Ben.

They were breathing hard. They had run back into the town from Talleyard's and the last mile had been painful. And they were wet. Much of their run had been in the rain. They walked quickly across the floor of the hall, heading for the far wall.

Reaching it, Lindsay ran her finger along the lines of school pictures.

'There,' she said, pointing.

Ben stood and, reaching forwards, carefully balanced Talleyard's photograph above those of 1935 and 1937. At first, it didn't seem to mean anything. And then Lindsay realized what was happening.

'Look at the lines,' she said quickly.

'The what?'

'They're standing in lines. The oldest and biggest at the back, the youngest at the front. In fact, that means they're probably standing in classes.'

Ben nodded, not quite sure what Lindsay was saying.

'Here, in 1935, look at this line. I don't know how old they are. Probably not very old. But count them.'

Ben scanned the line of fading faces. Solemn, except for the one at the end who was almost laughing.

'Ten.'

'And in 1936? On Talleyard's picture?'

'Eleven.'

'Exactly. They've been joined by the girl.'

'And now look at 1937.'

Ben's eyes shifted carefully to the next photograph, looking for the familiar line. It had gone. Where there had been ten people, then eleven, now there were only three. A pale girl and two boys.

Lindsay turned to Ben. 'That 1936 picture was probably the last ever picture taken of those kids.'

'What do you mean?'

'In 1936, seven of them disappeared. The names on the wall outside, Ben. They weren't some people on a pleasure cruise. Those names were the children. These children. But you can only see that when you put the three photographs together.'

Ben frowned.

'There's eleven kids in 1936. And three in 1937. That means eight of them disappeared.' He paused. 'But there's only seven names outside.'

Mrs Dodds had started rattling the doors, fiddling with the long bolts that would lock them. Lindsay looked at Ben, not quite believing what she was about to say.

'Ben. The eighth is still alive. We've seen her.'

10

From the churchyard, above the harbour, they could see Dan's boat slipping from its moorings and slowly turning its nose towards the open sea.

'His first day back,' said Ben, watching as his brother moved the boat through the water, picking up speed as he pulled into the more open waters of the estuary.

'I'm not sure I could do it,' said Lindsay. 'Not after what happened.'

Ben shrugged his shoulders. 'They say lightning never strikes in the same place twice.'

Lindsay could see someone moving about on the deck of the boat. It was probably Ahab. 'They also say that sharks don't attack people in England.'

She turned back towards Ben.

'We're putting it off.'

'I know,' said Ben. He leant down and lifted the catch of the small churchyard gate. The gate opened, creaking slightly as Ben pushed it.

They walked along the shingle path that

led to the church doors, locked now against the midday glare of the sun. The weather front of the previous day had moved on inland, taking the rain with it and leaving behind the clear blue skies of late July.

The churchyard was quiet. Here, the souls of long-dead villagers lay at peace, now at one with the rhythms of the natural world and with the silence that lies at its heart.

'Where do we start?' said Lindsay. She glanced over the rows of jumbled headstones. Some tall, others short. Some at an angle. Others lying on the ground. They might have been so many people, turning to see who their visitors might be.

'I don't know,' said Ben.

'Well, in that case,' said Lindsay, stepping off the path and on to the uneven grass that led to the graves, 'we might as well start with the first one we come to.'

It was Talleyard's grandfather. Taken from the rocks below the cliffs and buried beneath a simple stone.

William Talleyard. March 4th, 1919. Now with God. And with Jack.

'I wonder who Jack was?' said Ben.

Lindsay shook her head.

'It was obviously important to them at the time.' She glanced to her right at a second headstone.

Nathan Talleyard. Born December 2nd, 1902. Died, August 28th, 1946. All is forgiven. And forgotten.

They walked slowly on, stopping by each headstone, glancing at the name, the date. The ground beneath their feet was spongy, partly because of the rain, partly because of the dark patches of moss that were beginning to take over from the grass, like so many stains on a carpet. The sun was hot. Ben stopped, wiping the sweat off his forehead and looking back towards the church.

'I didn't think it would be so difficult.'

Behind the church and running up the hill beyond, there was a small wood, the trees now in the full leaf of summer, some moving in a slight breeze coming from the fields below. Rooks circled above the wood, aimlessly, listlessly.

'Well,' said Lindsay, 'the funny thing is that if you look in the haystack for long enough, you're bound to find the needle. Or, at least, one of them.'

'Needles?'

'Children. Look behind you.'

Ben turned quickly. He had stopped in front of a small grave, its sides marked out with roughly-cut stones, a small rusting metal vase which might have once held flowers in the centre and, at its head, a stubby, black marble headstone.

Ben read it aloud.

'Annie Hannaford. Died August 3rd, 1936. Aged 9. We can never forget you and we will be with you again soon, in Heaven. Bert and Nancy, your loving Mum and Dad.'

He fell silent. As a young boy, he had been vaguely aware of an old woman called Nancy Hannaford. He'd never spoken to her but he could remember the small, quiet woman who had seemed always to be dressed in black. He could see her now, scuttling up the main street, her head bent against the wind, a shawl wrapped tightly around her shoulders.

She was now lying beside her daughter.

Much earlier, to Annie's left, her father Bert had been buried. April 30th, 1938. He had not kept Annie waiting long.

'It may be just coincidence,' said Ben.

'Get serious, Ben,' said Lindsay, surprised by the sudden sharpness in her voice. 'Seven of them died in 1936 and they're all buried here. Somewhere.'

She knew he was frightened. She knew that, because she was frightened too.

They moved slowly on, both now silent in the presence of death and of the harsh reality that all too often lay beyond the simple words of a stone.

They found the next one just over ten minutes later. *John Dornom. Died August 3rd, 1936. Aged 9. Dearest and only son of John and Lily. You will be forever in our hearts.*

Lindsay felt the tears welling in her eyes. She had no idea who John and Lily Dornom might have been but she could imagine only too well the grief of losing their child at the age of nine. She thought of the children in the photograph, wondering which one had been John. The one on the left grinning, perhaps. Or the nervous one with his hat on sideways. Or even the one on the right, who looked as if he would break into laughter at any moment. Laughing Boy.

'God bless you,' she said softly and, turning to her right, moved slowly away from the grave.

Above the woods, the rooks had suddenly risen from the trees, no more drifting haphazardly through the air but now irritated, disturbed by something or somebody. Ben glanced up as he heard their screeching. It might have been anything. Even a fox.

'Shall we go back?' he called. He could see Lindsay shaking her head. There were tears on her cheeks when at last she turned back to him.

'No,' she said. 'We owe it to those children. For all these years, whatever happened to them has been a secret. Buried, like them. We owe it to them to tell their story, Ben. Nobody else is ever going to.'

Ben nodded. 'The only thing, Linds, is that we don't know it.'

He walked towards her, putting his arm around her shoulders. She let her head fall against him, the tears falling again now.

'Someone must know it, Ben,' she whispered. 'Someone.'

* * *

The man crossed the road above the church. He walked lazily, sometimes stopping to swing one boot round in a wide circle above the ground, watching the shadow follow it. As he did so, he laughed. And then walked on again.

Despite the heat of the day, he wore a long, dark coat. It was dirty, torn in several places and was tied around his waist with string. The cuffs of his shirt stuck out from the end of the coat-sleeves and his baggy trousers flapped about the top of his boots as he walked. His hair was long, its greying ends reaching down to his shoulders. On top of his head, he wore a fisherman's cap.

As he grew nearer to the graveyard, he stopped, cocking his head to one side, as if listening. He could hear nothing but the drone of the bees and the screeching of the rooks high above his head. He hadn't really meant to upset them but he'd been unable to stop himself from throwing a stick at one of them. He hadn't wanted to hurt it. It was just so funny when all these creatures started flapping their wings and chasing up into the sky.

Then he saw Lindsay and Ben.

He straightened his head, an expression of curiosity, even surprise, on his face. He had never seen these people before. He'd heard someone talking once about people called 'holiday-makers'. Perhaps these two were holiday-makers. He would find out.

Moving to the side of the road, he began to clamber over the dry-stone wall that ran along the northern edge of the church-yard. They still hadn't seen him.

He thought he would play a game. If he could get near them, perhaps even right up to them, without them knowing, he could jump out and scream and that would scare them. And that would be fun.

He began to slide from one gravestone to the next, every so often peering round their edges to make sure the holiday-makers hadn't run away. He moved quietly. Often, he had to do this when he was chasing rabbits. He knew how to move quietly, without being seen.

Lindsay had stopped crying. She lifted her head, wiping her eyes and then putting the tissue back in her pocket.

'I'm sorry,' she said. 'It's just that . . . '

'I know,' said Ben.

They stood quietly for some moments. Then Lindsay looked up. 'We need to find the others.'

Ben smiled. 'Sure.'

Neither of them had seen the man. Nor heard him. Suddenly, he was there. With a howl, he had thrown himself from behind a gravestone and now stood in front of them, his arms punching high in the air, his legs kicking out in all directions. And all the while he howled.

'What — ?' Ben quickly pulled Lindsay behind him, squaring up to the prancing figure facing him. His right fist clenched. In his left-hand pocket, his hand closed around some house keys.

And then, just as suddenly as he had started, the man stopped. And then began laughing, throwing his head back and roaring with deep-throated laughter.

'Ben . . .'

'Don't move,' whispered Ben. 'Wait and see what he does.'

The man stopped laughing and stood perfectly still, his eyes fixed on the two people in front of him.

'You didn't laugh,' he said, at last.

Ben shook his head.

'That's a shame,' said the man. 'I was hoping we could all have a laugh together.' He ran his coat-sleeve across his face. ' 'Tis hot today.'

No one moved. The rooks were settling back into the trees. Down in the harbour, a boat's horn sounded.

'An' so, you're holiday-makers then?' The man looked quizzically towards them.

'Not that I knows what a holiday-maker is. I can make soup. Rabbit soup. If I's catchin' rabbits. But I don't never heard of a holiday.'

He looked up at the church clock. 'How do you make it then?'

Ben began to reply, finding his voice at last.

'No, we're not — '

'That's going to start binging in a minute. You see if it don't. Bing. Bing. Bing. It's a terrific laugh.'

He continued to stare up at the clock. Faintly, Ben could hear the springs inside it beginning to uncoil. The minute hand clicked to its vertical position and the clock now began to chime the hour. The man started laughing, looking quickly back to Lindsay and Ben and then up again at the clock.

'You see?' he said, grinning from ear to ear. 'Told you. 'Tis really funny.'

When the chimes had finally died away, he stopped laughing. Once again he was looking at Lindsay and Ben. Lindsay took a step towards him. 'Do you live here?'

Instinct was telling her that the man meant no harm.

'Me?' The man pointed to himself with

an extravagant gesture. 'Do I live here? No, bless you. No, I don't live here. This is a church. Nobody lives here. Except them.' He waved his arms toward the gravestones. 'And they're no fun. I lives over there. Over them hills and behind them woods. That's where I is. In a little cave. 'Tis alright. Mind you, they'm used to be fun.'

'Who?' Lindsay watched as the man now turned his gaze back towards the graves.

'My friends. They'm used to be fun.'

'Which friends?'

'They'm all dead now. All gone.'

A distant look had crept into the man's face. He was no longer talking to Lindsay and Ben. He was watching games with hoops and balls and the shells of dead crabs as the children played up and down the dusty main street. He was listening to their laughter, the shouts of parents and the call of the gulls high above. Suddenly, he was running with them, chasing the dogs across the quayside, skimming pebbles across the waters of the harbour, hurling themselves across the beaches and the fields and through the woods and finally tumbling home, helpless with laughter and covered in dirt as the sun slowly began to sink behind the cliffs on the western skyline, bringing the day to a close.

'What's your name?' Ben's quiet voice broke into the brief dream. The man turned, his eyes misty.

'My name?' He smiled. 'They call me Laughing Boy.'

11

Talleyard stood in front of the hearth, looking at the photograph on the mantelpiece in front of him.

A tall man, standing outside an ivy-covered doorway, a book in one hand, a walking cane in the other. He was wearing a blazer and although he was attempting a smile, it was clear that his natural pose would be one of formality.

'Don't worry, father,' Talleyard said quietly. 'I won't let you down.'

He turned and left the room, closing the door behind him. In the corner of the kitchen, the cat opened one eye and then settled back to sleep. It was too hot outside to leave the cool stone floor. It was on that stone floor that they had laid Talleyard's father when they had cut him down. He had been hanging from one of the kitchen beams.

At sixty-two, Talleyard could no longer climb the cliff steps as quickly as he might have liked. Not that he had ever been especially active. Apart from fishing, he'd never been very interested in sport. He had no interest in how he looked or in how he felt and any thought of a regular routine of exercises would have horrified him. By the time he reached the top of the steps, he was out of breath.

He looked out over the sea. It was calm, a deep blue reflecting the colour of the skies above. He nodded slowly in its direction, as if in approval. And then turned away and began walking. The path he now took led him away from the cliffs and down towards a valley that lay some two miles inland. Nobody lived there. No roads led to it. None led through it. The family that had farmed the land around it for over two hundred years had never attempted to clear it and the result was a confusion of woodland, fern and bramble, clinging precariously to the steep valley sides. At its bottom, a thin, bubbling stream twisted its way through the tangle, a distant relative of the river that had once carved the valley through the hard stone of the hills.

He walked steadily, a small brown wicker basket hanging from a strap round his shoulders, swinging backwards and forwards as he marched on. He was alone on the path. Few people even knew about the valley and the chance visitor, happening upon it by accident, would almost always turn away at the first sight of its dark, unwelcoming depths.

For Talleyard, it had become a refuge. He knew the creatures that lived there, the plants that grew there. He knew the winding tracks made by the foxes, the clearings made by the badgers. He knew the sounds of the insects that destroyed either themselves or each other. He knew that he would find what he was looking for and he knew where he would find them.

It was just past midday when he reached the edges of the valley. Now he was alone, deep in the countryside, listening to the gentle cooing of woodpigeons and chatter of small birds as they played in the branches above.

He began to climb down the sloping valley side. The path quickly gave way to an untidy, overgrown latticework of long, gangling weeds, threading their way through spindly, wild bushes and the branches of fallen trees. The ground was soft with the mulch of layer upon layer of leaves that fell each year and rotted where they lay. Talleyard continued his descent. He had found a fox-trail and was now following it as it curled down the slope towards the stream. As the sun above was now lost, so the peace of the valley took over, an almost cathedral-like solemnity that closed out all noise other than the immediate call of a bird sounding a note of alarm or the shiver of dead grasses as a rabbit ran through them.

Some yards short of the stream, Talleyard stopped, crouching low behind a thick screen of tall, green ferns. He tried to breathe slowly, quietly. To his right, something moved. And then stopped. He turned his head. At first, he couldn't see it, its body and legs dark against the shadows of the valley floor. And then it moved again. Quickly. Stopping just beyond Talleyard's reach. Its dark eyes seemed to glitter as it now sat watching him. Talleyard studied it for a few moments.

When his father had first shown him one of the wood spiders of the valley, he'd been terrified. The creatures had crawled into his dreams for days afterwards, clawing at him, their thick legs curling round his neck. He remembered waking up screaming, night after night, his screams echoing through the small dark rooms of the coastguard's cottage.

But he had learnt to live with them. Over the years, whenever he'd seen them, they had never attacked him. Or shown any inclination to. They had seemed content to simply sit and watch him, curious perhaps as to the identity or intentions of their visitor.

Now Talleyard turned away again, looking ahead through the sloping trees of the valley. He edged forwards, pushing the ferns to one side but still keeping low to the ground, his senses alert to any unfamiliar sound or movement. The spider followed him. He fell to his knees, finding it easier to crawl as he now burrowed into the thickening tangle of bramble bushes in front of him. Beyond them lay a clearing, the stream running along one side and single shafts of sunlight spreading down from the blanket of leaves above to the matted grass of the valley floor.

Suddenly, Talleyard caught his breath. He was perfectly still, grateful for the protection of the brambles. Hidden deep inside their shadows, he could not be seen. He'd seen the brief flash of white in the trees at the far side of the clearing. It hadn't been an animal.

He waited.

Behind him, he could hear something scratching at the leaves of the bushes. He knew it was the spider. His gaze remained on the clearing, not knowing quite what to expect but knowing that he was no longer alone.

The girl appeared quite suddenly, stepping quickly out of the shadows of the trees, the white of her long dress caught in a shaft of sunlight.

Talleyard froze, breathing slowly through his mouth. Lying on the ground, he seemed almost to be willing himself to become a part of it as he flattened himself amongst the dark rotting leaves.

The girl was now wandering around the clearing. She seemed to be looking for something, her eyes never leaving the ground. Her face was expressionless, her skin pale, her deep red hair falling over her shoulders and swaying gently as she walked.

The same face, the same skin, the same hair that had floated beneath the surface of the pool. Then she stopped. She had seen something by the base of the thin silver birch that grew somewhat clumsily at the far side of the clearing. Its trunk was twisted, its back arched almost as if in pain. The girl moved towards the trunk, staring at the ground. She leant forwards.

When she screamed, it was a sound that seemed to reach into the very edges of Talleyard's soul. It seemed to echo through the trees and slopes of the valley, a hideous, hollow screeching that followed her now as she turned, stumbling and clawing her way across the grass, desperate to reach the safety of the trees. And then she was gone.

And slowly the sound faded, as the traces of a nightmare recede with the coming of the day. Talleyard remained hidden for some minutes after the girl had disappeared, his heart now slowing, his breathing more even. When at last it seemed the girl would not return, he edged slowly forwards again, emerging from the bramble thicket on the edges of the clearing.

He stood, brushing the damp leaves from his clothes with his hands. The wicker basket still hung from his shoulder. Slowly, he began to walk across the grass, still glancing into the trees, fearful that she might reappear. He knew what she had found. He smiled. So the old stories were true, after all.

He reached the silver birch and looked down. The snake was coiled, the patterns of its skin pulsing as the creature breathed, its thick body furled in upon itself. Its cold eyes watched Talleyard, a sharp tongue flickered out of its mouth and above its shallow forehead the dark V of its birthmark glowed in the sunlight. The birthmark of the adder.

⋆ ⋆ ⋆

'I don't care what you say. She doesn't care what you say. In fact, nobody, except possibly you, cares what you say, so will you please simply get out of my way and let me go and find her.'

Ben's father glared at the doctor standing in front of him. A porter passed them, wheeling a short metal bed down the hospital corridor.

'Mr Carson, your mother-in-law's very ill.'

'She is now.'

'What's that supposed to mean?'

'Before she came in here, she was

perfectly well. Apart from a bang on the side of the head when she fell over.'

'Mr Carson, she was delirious.'

'Don't talk nonsense.'

'She'd seen what she thought — '

'And whatever you do, don't start telling me a whole lot of rubbish about ghosts and things that go bump in the middle of the night because if you do, I shall almost certainly take that pot over there and break it over your head. Now, please, just tell me where I can find her.'

Ben's father paused, waiting for the other man to reply. The phone call had come from Phoebe no more than an hour before. In a rather desperate voice, she'd said that if she was going to die, she wanted to die at home. As far as John Carson was concerned, if everything she'd said was true, then her home seemed a great deal safer anyway. He didn't believe all Ben's nonsense about little girls that disappeared and dogs that went mad as soon as it started raining, but he did believe the fear that he'd heard in the old woman's voice.

The doctor stood to one side. 'If anything happens . . . '

'I know.'

'You'll find her in Room 54. We moved her yesterday.'

* * *

Ben watched from the Land Rover as his father emerged from the main doors of the hospital, Phoebe clinging to his arm. Moments later, a porter followed them, carrying a suitcase. Getting out, Ben ran across the car park to meet them.

'Hi, Gran.'

'Hello, Ben.'

He kissed her and then, as she walked on with his father, he waited for the porter. 'Don't worry, I'll take that.' He pointed to the suitcase. Harry smiled and handed it to him.

'Look after her, won't you? She's had a nasty shock. Maybe your dad's right. Maybe she will be better off at home.'

Ben took the case. 'And you still don't know what happened?'

'Not really.'

'You said she saw something.'

'She thought she saw something.' Harry paused. 'Only she couldn't have done.'

'Why not?'

'She said it was a face. A girl. I saw . . .' He stopped.

'You saw it?' said Ben.

'But I couldn't have done,' said Harry. 'It must have been a reflection or something.'

'Why?'

Harry paused for a moment, seeing the girl once again at the back of his mind.

'That window's forty feet from the ground. A sheer drop. There's no way anyone could have been outside it.'

'Anyone, maybe,' said Ben, starting to walk back towards the car. 'But not anything.'

* * *

'Will you be all right, Phoebe?'

Tom Walker's voice was quiet, his smile kind as he sat on the other side of the fire.

'Oh, I should think so,' said Phoebe, her hands around a cup of coffee as she sat and stared into the glowing coals of the fire. She was glad to be back in her home. 'Dorothy's coming over in a little while.' She would be pleased to see her daughter.

At the other side of the creek, the setting sun was now bathing the trees and fields in dull, orange light. Tom looked at his watch.

'I'll wait for her.'

'No, no, it's all right.' Phoebe looked up. 'I can cope.'

'No, I don't think you can,' said Tom, suddenly. 'I don't think any of us can.'

He hadn't wanted to say anything. He'd wanted to leave his worst fears buried, as far away as possible from the imagination and dreams of his old friend who sat opposite him. 'I'm sorry, I didn't . . . '

'It's all right, Tom,' said Phoebe gently. 'I already know she's back.'

'You know?'

'I've seen her. Twice.' She sipped her coffee. 'I always knew she'd come back for us.'

'Shouldn't have happened,' said Tom, slowly. 'But someone took the lid off the coffin.'

'You've seen it?' Phoebe was staring at Tom.

'We had to be sure. Donald, that is. And me.'

'So the villagers really did it? All those years ago.'

Tom looked back towards the old woman. There had almost been a note of pride in her voice.

'Yes, Phoebe. They really did.'

12

Tom walked briskly.

He would have preferred to have had Donald's company but there had been no answer at his cottage. Tom wondered whether or not he should have waited until he'd found his friend. Another day wouldn't have made any difference. Instead of this, he could now have been with Lindsay, who'd said she was going walking in the hills beyond the church. More fun, surely, than walking alone, to find someone he'd never wanted to see.

To his left, the waters of the estuary shimmered in the morning sunshine. The hill rose away from the water and, as he climbed, slowly the estuary's full length came into view, the harbour at one end, the open sea at the other. Somewhere, far down the road behind him, he could hear the sound of a car being driven too quickly.

In his right hand, he carried his stick. Many years before, he had made it out of a piece of driftwood he'd found floating at the edges of Gerston beach. It had splintered when Tom had so wildly and so hopelessly flailed out with it at the child, only to bring it crashing into the rock, but it had not broken. Rather than lose an old friend, Tom had taped it and he now carried it before him, almost as a good luck charm. A relic of the real world where, despite all the odds, good somehow prevailed. He wondered whether or not good was all that was needed.

* * *

The gates were now in view. As Tom reached the driveway, he remembered Lindsay. Remembered her telling him of how she and Ben had rested against them when they'd first arrived, drinking water in the heat of the day. Tom rather wished he'd had the sense to pack a bottle.

But, as he turned towards the drive itself and the low-slung tapestry of branches that hung overhead, his thoughts left the real world and once more stood poised on the edges of the twilight universe, where the very worst dreams come true and where the very best ones falter. He began to walk slowly down the drive. Where, a few nights ago, he had walked with purpose, knowing exactly where he was going, what he wanted to do, he now ambled, almost as if waiting for something to happen.

He reached the pines, rounding the corner to see the ruins of the house in front of him. He stood still, watching, waiting. Nothing happened. He began walking again, the soles of his boots crunching on the gravel. His eyes wandered from one corner of the garden to another, his gaze sweeping the untended wilderness for signs of life. He reached the edge of the lawn and looked across to the large, spreading cedar tree.

And then somewhere, faintly, he heard the sound of laughter.

* * *

Lindsay had little or no idea of where she was going. Laughing Boy had simply said 'over the hills and behind the woods'. He might just as well have said over the hills and far away.

She'd passed the church and skirted round the edges of the rooks' wood. There were no paths. She was simply walking across the fields. Occasionally, one or two of the cows that stood quietly chewing on the grass would look up at her, their large brown eyes following her as she walked by.

He had spoken of a cave.

Behind the woods, the ground dipped sharply towards a small creek. Beyond the creek, there was a short, shingle beach, partly covered with black, rotting seaweed. As she made her way down the slope, she could also see the bare wooden ribs of a small boat that, over the years, had slowly disintegrated, leaving only its bones at the water's edge.

She reached the creek. It was too deep to wade through.

'I always swims it.'

The voice was loud, sudden. Lindsay screamed. He was behind her. She turned quickly. Laughing Boy simply threw back his head and shook with laughter.

'No, I doesn't really,' he said, when he finally stopped. 'I'm telling lies. Really, I just walks round it. Watch.' He started walking along the side of the creek. Then he stopped. And turned back to Lindsay. 'You coming? I got a piece of turnip we could share.'

She nodded and followed him.

The creek was not as long as it had looked and they were soon standing on the shingle of the beach. The seaweed, some still moist to the touch, smelt rancid, but further up the beach, a small stick fire burned, bringing the sweeter smell of wood-smoke into the air. Beyond the fire, set into the low rock face that ran underneath the fields above, Lindsay could see the cave. Drawn partly across its front was an old carpet, hanging from a rope that stretched from the exposed roots of trees that stood at either side of the cave's entrance. Like guardian soldiers.

Laughing Boy appeared from behind the curtain.

In one hand, he held a knife. In the other, a large piece of dirty turnip.

'We'll sit then, shall we?' he said. 'Sit by the fire an' play at grown-ups.' He started chuckling. 'Grown-ups, eh? That'd be a laugh.'

Still grinning, he sat down by the fire. Lindsay sat down too. It all reminded her of a book she'd had to read at school years before. About some children who went off and lived on islands and sat round campfires. They'd also been pretending to be grown-ups.

Laughing Boy cut off a rough piece of turnip and handed it to Lindsay. She took it.

'Came from that farm over there.' He jerked his thumb briefly back over his shoulder. 'They won't miss it.'

'Have you always lived here?' said Lindsay.

'Here? No.' Laughing Boy looked at her sideways as he began to chew on his piece of turnip. 'Been all over the world, me. Knew I'd end up here though.'

'Didn't you miss your friends when you went away?'

'Friends? Laughing Boy got friends? I got no friends.'

'What happened to them?'

Laughing Boy said nothing. Lindsay realized that she had gone too far. Slowly, he put down his knife and the piece of turnip and, getting up, walked back towards his cave. As he reached it, he took hold of the carpet, about to pull it across and close out the world. He looked down the short beach at Lindsay.

'Was that girl! She done it!' His voice was hoarse. 'Laughing Boy got no friends!'

He closed the curtain. Lindsay got up and carefully walked to the cave. Where there had once been laughter, she could now hear only the sound of tears.

* * *

Tom knew that she would find him. He stepped on to the lawn. He looked toward the house, almost as if seeking approval, but the crumbling shell seemed simply to stare past him and up into the sky.

Something behind him moved. He turned quickly. A small squirrel was sitting on its hind legs, clutching a berry in its paws. It watched him, keeping very still, hoping the man wouldn't see him. Then it blinked. And quickly putting the berry into its mouth, it turned and scampered away towards the bushes. Tom smiled, watching it go.

When he turned to face the cedar tree again, she was there. Standing beneath the tree, beside the two gravestones. Her hands clasped together in front of her, her head tilted slightly to one side.

Tom now felt the chill that Ben had described. The chill of a winter's morning on a summer's day. She began to walk towards him. As she did so, she smiled. Tom didn't move.

'Hello,' she said, stopping in front of him.

Tom said nothing. Fear was now tightening its fingers round his throat.

Her eyes were black, her skin so pale it was almost transparent. Her nostrils flared slightly. Long blue veins rans down the sides of her neck. She wore a long white dress, which had begun to fray at the edges and at the seams.

'Have you come for my party?'

Still Tom was silent. He wanted to speak. To scream. But he could do nothing.

'You were very naughty last time,' said the girl, her black eyes still fixed on him. 'You and your friends missed it.'

'I . . . er . . .' His words were halting, painful. He could feel the bile welling in his throat.

'Well, don't miss it this time, will you?' The girl's smile had gone. Her teeth now appeared behind her thin lips as she spoke. 'It's on Friday. When the sun's gone away. And if you miss it, Eve will be very cross. And I'll do something very nasty.'

And suddenly she screeched, opening her mouth wide, the rows of pointed teeth gleaming white in vicious contrast to the dark recesses of her throat. The screech burst through every fibre of Tom's body. Falling to his knees, he was violently sick, his head spinning, his whole body shaking. He slumped forward on to the earth and suddenly all went dark.

* * *

Lindsay was walking across the fields. She'd said she was going near the church. And there it was. Not far away. And there were the woods, the rooks circling above them. And there, standing quietly in the field, chewing the grass were the cows. But they'd gone. Where were they? Where were the cows? Lindsay was still walking, walking toward the church. Where was Ben? Ah, yes, Ben was fishing with his brother. That's why Lindsay was alone. That's why Lindsay . . . but where were the cows? They were always in the field. It was the right field, wasn't it? Yes, it was. There was the church. And now Lindsay's walking down towards the stone wall. And what's happening up there? The cows. They're all together. They're all standing at the top of the hill together and now they're all running down it together. Running down it together. Running towards Lindsay. And getting faster. And bellowing. And Lindsay's running but she can't run fast enough. And they're going to catch her and she's running. And then they've caught her. And they're flinging her into the stone wall. And trampling on her. And kicking her. And bursting through the stone wall and running away. And Lindsay's lying on the ground. And Lindsay's not moving. Lindsay's dead. And, as her blood seeped into the warm earth, the distant laughter began.

* * *

Tom's eyes opened. The girl had gone. Now the gardens were empty again. The warmth of the sun had returned.

Painfully, he pulled himself to his feet, his right arm numb, his shoulder hurting where he had fallen. He shook his head, ridding himself of the nightmare. And then he remembered.

Friday.

* * *

As she sat and watched him, she could see that he was slowly falling asleep.

'Grandad.'

Tom woke, sitting back in his chair with a start, his eyes blinking. Then he settled once more, looking across the top of his glasses towards Lindsay.

'Grandad, I think it's time you went to bed.'

Tom smiled and glanced towards the old clock that stood on the shelf by the door. It was just after nine o'clock.

'I haven't finished my coffee yet.'

He twisted in the chair and reached for the small brown mug that was sitting on the table beside him. Lifting it to his mouth, he sipped quietly, thoughtfully.

'Grandad, you still haven't told me how you hurt yourself.'

Lindsay had knelt down again beside the fire, looking up at her grandfather.

'Just fell over,' he said, distantly, putting the mug back down on the table. 'I suppose it's no more than getting old.'

'Maybe,' said Lindsay, quietly. It might explain the bruises but it didn't explain the fear in his eyes. She watched the small reflected flames dancing on the polished sides of the brass coal bucket. She knew he wasn't going to say any more. 'How was Ben's grandma the other night?'

'Phoebe?'

Tom smiled gently, thinking of the old woman, surrounded by pictures of her long-dead husband. 'Oh, she'll be all right. Phoebe's a survivor.' He was gazing deep into the coals of the fire.

'Grandad, I . . . '

Lindsay had wanted to ask him about Laughing Boy. About the children buried in the churchyard. About Talleyard's photograph. But the old man was now looking at her sadly and, as he watched her, Lindsay could see the tears welling in the corners of each eye.

'Lindsay.'

'Yes, Grandad?'

'If anything ever happened to me . . . '

'Don't be silly, Grandad.'

'But if it did.'

'What kind of 'anything'?'

'You would know that I always loved you. That I always tried to do my best for you. You would know that, wouldn't you? You'd remember these simple words?'

Lindsay smiled and held out her hand to him. 'Of course I would, Grandad. And they're not simple. They're lovely.'

13

There was a small vole in the first trap.

Talleyard bent down and peered at it. Having squeezed its way into the plastic tube, attracted by the small square of chocolate, the animal had unwittingly triggered a spring behind it. Now, it could do no more than run the length of the tube, stopping only to stare out at the world beyond.

'That's one,' muttered Talleyard, opening the tube and dropping the small, furry animal into a glass jar.

He had placed the second trap beside the strawberries. Even in the late summer, there were still some growing there and they would have attracted the small creatures of the night. As he approached it, Talleyard could see something moving inside. It wasn't a vole. Or even a mouse. Looking more closely, he saw that he had caught a small frog. 'It'll have to do,' he said to himself and, unscrewing the top, tipped the small creature into the glass jar, along with the vole.

The basket was at the front of the house, carefully stored beneath the bench on which Talleyard would sometimes sit on long summer evenings, watching over the sea. They would have some protection there and the basket itself was well made. Reaching it, he knelt and began to pull it out. As he did so, he noticed two figures making their way down the cliffside approach to the cottage. He thought it was probably the two kids.

Once it was clear of the bench, Talleyard undid the two leather buckles that held the top down and, opening it very slightly, he peered inside.

He smiled. 'Breakfast.'

Dropping the lid again, he reached for the jar and unscrewed the top. 'Sorry about this. But it's called the law of the jungle, I'm afraid.'

Again, he lifted the lid, this time wider, and with a swift move of his hand, he tipped the contents of the jar into the basket. He did it quickly, giving the creatures inside no time to realize what was happening. Snapping the lid shut again, he fastened the buckles and slid the basket back beneath the bench. He could hear the banging of the metal knocker on the kitchen door.

'I'm coming!' he shouted.

Straightening up again, he smiled briefly. The frog and the vole would last them a few days. Which was probably all that was needed.

* * *

'How much do you know?' said Lindsay.

Talleyard lit his pipe, standing with his back to the empty fireplace.

'About what?'

'About those children.'

'Children?'

'The ones who died in August, 1936,' said Ben. 'These children.' He pulled Talleyard's photograph from the cloth bag he'd been carrying over his shoulder.

Talleyard drew on his pipe, blowing thin blue smoke into the still air of the small cottage room. At first he said nothing. Then he glanced across to the window. There was a space on the wall beside it, where the photograph had been.

'The ones buried in the churchyard,' said Lindsay. 'The ones with the names above the town hall door. Those children.'

Still Talleyard said nothing.

'And who's the girl?' said Ben. 'The one you were going to kill.'

Lindsay put her photograph down on the small table in the centre of the room. 'Is that where she lived?'

Talleyard leant forwards, taking the pipe out of his mouth and looking carefully at the picture. The girl was standing at the top of the steps that led into the ruined house. He looked up. He was trying not to show it but Lindsay knew that they had struck a nerve. When he spoke, Talleyard's voice was low, cold.

'Where did you get that?'

'I took it,' said Lindsay. She was watching him carefully. 'Who is she?'

Talleyard turned away from them, walking slowly across to the small windows that looked out over the garden and the sea. He could see the basket still under the bench. It seemed to be moving slightly.

'I can't tell you,' he said slowly. He didn't look at them.

'Why not?' said Ben.

'Because it isn't my story to tell.'

'Whose is it?'

'The ones who were there. And the ones who survived.'

'But you know what happened?'

Talleyard turned and looked at them. 'Yes.'

'Then why . . . ?'

'Because I made a promise to that man over there. That's why.' He nodded in the direction of the mantlepiece. The silver frame holding the image of a man, half-smiling and wearing a striped blazer.

'Who's he?' said Lindsay.

'My father.'

Lindsay remembered the second headstone. Nathan Talleyard. Father of Brian. Lying alongside his father William, who was now with God, and with Jack.

'It's all forgotten now, anyway,' said Talleyard softly, relighting his pipe. 'And it was all a very long time ago.'

'But what about the girl?' said Ben. 'She's not a long time ago. She's here and now.'

Talleyard shook his head slowly.

'An illusion. Just something that you think you've seen.'

'And the photograph?'

'Photograph?'

'This one. The one Lindsay took.'

Ben picked the picture up from the table. And then felt the chill run down the back of his neck as he looked at it. The steps in front of the house were empty. The girl was no longer there.

* * *

Ben said nothing as they walked back towards the town. He was frightened. He had been prepared to accept that the girl might have been an illusion. That she hadn't appeared when they'd visited the ruins. That it hadn't been her face at the window of his grandmother's house. That the dog had been driven mad by the storm. And that whatever happened in 1936 was, as Talleyard had said, something that was 'all a long time ago'.

But he had seen the photograph several times. In the cold light of day. Lindsay had seen it. It had existed. The girl had been standing on the top of the steps. And suddenly, she had gone.

'Linds, I'm not sure . . . '

Lindsay stopped. She could feel the afternoon sun, warm on her back. Beneath the coast road they had taken were the sounds of children on the beaches below that now drifted up towards them.

'Ben, do you remember what he said

when you asked him whose story it was to tell?'

Ben stood in the middle of the road, his mind running over their conversation with Talleyard.

'Yes. The ones who'd been there.'

'And the ones who survived.'

'Something like that.'

Lindsay's eyes were bright, the sound of her grandfather's words now ringing clearly above the sounds of the summer afternoon.

'Phoebe's a survivor, Ben, that's what Grandad said. That's the word he used. 'Survivor'.'

'There was three of them,' said Ben, suddenly, the pictures on the library wall coming sharply back into focus. 'In 1937, the year after, there was three of them left. Two boys. One girl.'

Lindsay watched him carefully.

'Phoebe?'

'I don't know,' said Ben. 'But we can always ask.'

* * *

It seemed odd to open Phoebe's gate and not hear Edison barking. Even if he hadn't entirely believed Ben and his stories about the girl, Ben's father had still felt it better to be safe rather than sorry and the dog had been sent to some nearby kennels. He didn't want Phoebe having any more surprises.

Not that it stopped Ben from raising the ghosts of the past, as they sat with Phoebe in her cottage garden, watching as the late afternoon sun began to throw longer and longer shadows across the waters of the creek.

'Gran, who was Laughing Boy?'

The old woman was startled. She hadn't heard that name for over sixty years.

'I don't . . . '

She hesitated. Ben watched her carefully. If he was right. If his grandmother was the girl in the photograph of 1937, one of the three who had survived whatever had happened, then she would know exactly who Laughing Boy was. And she wouldn't lie to him. Ben knew that. So did Phoebe.

'Laughing Boy?'

Phoebe now smiled, sitting back in her wooden garden-chair, her mind going back to the young boy who had never seemed to stop laughing. An infectious laugh. A laugh that no one could ever resist. Not even the teachers when they'd been trying their very best to be annoyed with him for getting his tables wrong, yet again.

'He never did like work,' she said, lifting her cup of tea from its saucer and sipping thoughtfully. 'I know that much. He always knew he was going to follow in his dad's footsteps and be a fisherman and he could never see the point of doing all this reading and writing. Wasn't necessary. He already knew more or less everything he needed to know about fishing, so why fiddle about in classrooms? That was his view.' She put the cup back down again. 'Maybe he was right. I don't know.'

'We met him,' said Lindsay. 'I've even been to see where he lives.'

'Met him?' The old woman jerked her head towards Lindsay. 'What do you mean, you've met him? You can't have. He's been dead for years.'

'No, he hasn't,' said Lindsay, softly. 'He's alive.'

Phoebe started shaking her head. The last time she'd seen the boy had been at the funerals. He had been standing very quietly at one side, near the gate. Nobody had been taking any notice of him when suddenly, he'd screamed, leapt over the wall and started running up the narrow road. It had been the last anybody had ever seen of him.

Years later, rumours surfaced that he'd been seen at the fish market in Plymouth but they had been quickly forgotten. And, in time, it had only been the older villagers who had ever even heard of Laughing Boy. And they had long since vowed never to talk about the children again. Phoebe had been interested, briefly, in the rumours. She'd always been fond of the boy. But, like the others, she had done nothing, finally believing also that he must be dead.

'Alive?'

Lindsay nodded. 'With the mind of a child. But still alive.'

Phoebe looked across towards the trees on the far side of the creek, still bathed in the afternoon sun. 'Did he say anything?'

'Yes, he did.' Lindsay was thinking of the cave, of the sound of an old man crying in the darkness.

'He said the girl did it.'

Phoebe nodded slowly.

'So she did.'

Ben looked at her, sensing that his

grandmother had taken the decision to tell a story Talleyard had felt now belonged only to those who had died. And to those who had survived.

He spoke softly. 'Did what, Gran? What did she do?'

14

They had first appeared in the Spring of that year.

When the daffodils were coming out. And the bluebells in the woods. They had been called Hingis. Two parents, one child. A little girl.

As she sat back now, letting her mind drift over the years, Phoebe could see the tall, gaunt figure of the school's headmaster showing the family round the school. Not that there had been much of it to see. There had only been three teachers. The headmaster, Miss Penarth and a curiously fresh-faced young man who played the piano for the morning's assembly. There were four classrooms. And a playground at the back of the buildings where the grass had long been worn down to bare earth.

The Hingises had been introduced to Phoebe's class. They had moved into a large house up by the cliffs and now Eve was to join their year. Miss Penarth had said that one more would make eleven and wouldn't that be odd? But no one had laughed. Except Laughing Boy.

Eve had been quiet as the headmaster talked about her. Her long red hair had been tied by her mother into tight bunches at the back of her head. Her face was white. She didn't smile.

Two days later, she had started. At first, her mother would walk down to the school with her, unsmiling. Then she had stopped, leaving the girl to wander down alone. She was often late. Not that it seemed to bother her. When Miss Penarth had once raised her voice to her, Eve spat at her.

She rarely spoke to the other children, living in a world of her own. She took no interest in the lessons, spending her time gazing out of the windows or drawing wild, strange patterns on the pages of her books. During the various breaks, she would often be seen grubbing around in the hedge that ran along one side of the school grounds. She looked for spiders. Beetles. Caterpillars. Whatever she found, she would squeeze between her fingers and then drop into her mouth. She made no friends. But, in turn, she bothered nobody. Until one day, a young boy called

Lol Harris had approached her in the playground.

'You looking for bugs again, are you?'

Kneeling by the hedge, Eve had looked up. She hadn't spoken.

'My dad says what you do is disgusting,' said Lol. 'Eating creepy-crawlies. Says it makes him sick to hear about it.'

Eve still said nothing.

'Anyway, if you really want something horrible, try this.' And Lol had reached into his pocket and pulled out a worm which he then dropped down the back of Eve's dress.

She stood up, her eyes fixed on the boy in front of her. And then, quite suddenly, she had screamed at him, her mouth opening wide, revealing the teeth.

Lol had run back into the classroom where he had stayed for the rest of the day.

Some days later, his father and a group of other fishermen, had been sailing out towards the first of a series of crab pots, just over a mile off the coast. The wind had been light and the boats made little headway against the incoming tide. And yet the sun was hot, the sky blue. There had seemed little need to hurry.

Arthur Harris had been fishing since the

First World War. He'd fought in northern France but had been sent home after getting half his right foot blown off by a mortar-bomb. He'd been married, there were three children and Lol was the youngest.

The five boats drifted on across the shiny, blue surface of the sea, the wind barely moving the sails at the back of each one.

'Don't reckon as we'll get there before Christmas at this rate!' Arthur had shouted across to the nearest boat.

His neighbour had laughed. And then the laughter had choked in his throat.

Harris had been standing at the front of his boat, the upper half of his body clearly visible above the low wooden rail that ran around its sides. Where the sea at the side of his boat had been calm, there had now suddenly erupted from it a towering spray of foam and water, almost entirely engulfing the boat's deck and having, at its centre, the largest fish the man had ever seen. He saw enough of the frightening, jerking black shape to know it as a shark. He saw it rear high into the air and then fall on the screaming silhouette of Harris, the screams suddenly cut short as the fish took him in its jaws and fell back into the water, crashing against the side of the boat as it did so. Harris was never seen again.

Torn and bloodied swatches of clothing were found some days later, washed ashore on the sand of North Beach but a body was never found. They buried an empty coffin.

* * *

'And you think she made the shark do that?'

Ben tried not to let his disbelief sound too obvious.

'I don't know what I think,' said Phoebe, pulling her shawl closer to her as a gentle late afternoon breeze began to blow down the creek. 'I didn't then and I still don't.'

'But how could she?' said Lindsay.

'They said she had powers over the creatures.' Phoebe glanced across at her and looked away, almost as if embarrassed. 'They said she was a wreccan.'

'A what?'

'A country spirit. A devil. Sent to bring misery into the world.'

'Gran, I . . . '

'Don't say anything, Ben.' Phoebe's voice was steady. 'It doesn't matter whether you believe in such things or not. What mattered was that they did.'

She could remember the old country ways only too well. The corn dollies that were burnt to bring bad luck. The mackerel thrown alive on to the fire to protect the family from Satan calling in the night, the curious markings on the fish's back being known to be the first words of the Bible. The cutting of a lamb's throat in an open field to guarantee fine weather for the harvest.

In such a world, a wreccan could exist.

* * *

For some weeks, nothing more was heard of the girl. The school finished for the summer holiday. The older children went to help in the fields or on the boats. Those of Phoebe's age looked forward to several weeks of little more than playing from dawn till dusk, revelling in the uncomplicated joy of simply being children, running free beneath a summer sun.

The invitations had been sent to the headmaster. They were handwritten and tucked into neat, brown envelopes. Each had the name of the child for whom it was meant, written in careful, bold letters across the front.

William. Lizzie. John. Harry. In turn, each of the children in Phoebe's class had been invited. Even Lol Harris.

The headmaster knew who they were from but he didn't, at first, understand why they'd been given to him — left outside the front door of his small cottage, one morning late in July.

Then it became clear.

Eve had run away. She'd been laughed at in the playground and she hadn't felt able to come back to school in case they all started laughing again. This was her way of trying to make friends. Inviting her class to a party and hoping that, away from the school, it might be easier for her.

It had probably been her parents' idea. They'd also have guessed that sending the invitations directly to the children might not have worked. After all, none of them knew Eve. If anything, they were probably a little afraid of her. So, they'd clearly hoped that by involving the headmaster in handing them out, the class would be more likely to respond.

As he tied his boots, preparing to go out with the envelopes, the headmaster reflected that it was a kind idea. It would help Eve settle in, and what better for the children in summer than a party?

If it had been the parents' idea to involve the headmaster, they had been right. The initial reaction of the townsfolk to the invitations was one of reluctance. The families had heard about the strange girl who ate beetles and spat at teachers. They knew she'd screamed at Lol Harris and that she'd run away. She didn't seem the sort of child that their own children should be mixing with.

But the headmaster was very persuasive. As he stood at each front door, he argued that it was no more than a cry for help. Eve was almost certainly lonely, isolated. She'd been made to look foolish in the playground and it had frightened her. Now she was trying to say sorry. To be friends. It was all quite clear and although perhaps a little unusual, it was understandable. And the families had been persuaded.

The children themselves had been intrigued. They had never known what to make of Eve. It was odd that she should suddenly want to invite them to a party at her house but if they were all going, then why not?

Two days before the party, three of the children went down with heavy colds. Phoebe and two of the boys. In Phoebe's case, her mother said it was because she'd been swimming in the creek for far too long and hadn't come out when she'd been told to. It was all her own fault and there was no question of her going to any parties. She had a temperature of a hundred and one degrees and, despite the heat of the midsummer days, Phoebe was shivering as she lay in her small bed.

The night before the party, she had cried herself to sleep. By now, everyone had been getting very excited about the invitations and she was going to miss everything. Her tears were hot as they rolled down her cheeks and, as she slowly fell to sleep, she hoped that she might never wake up again.

The first day of August dawned with a blood-red sun. Heading their small boats out of the harbour, the fishermen looked back towards the east and knew they would be foolish to stay out at sea too long. The skies told of storms before the day was out.

Not that any such prospect had worried the children. They had all been up early. The invitation had been for the whole day, finishing with tea in the garden, and so, by ten o'clock, a short line of children were to be found winding their way up the hill leading from the small town centre to the cliffs. There were one or two mothers with them, although they had promised not to stay. The house had been strangely quiet when they arrived. There were no ribbons, no balloons, no squeaky gramophone playing in the background.

The group had walked slowly down to the house, many of them seeing it for the first time. The walls were covered with ivy, the chimneys so tall that they seemed to reach into the sky. The windows at the front were open and occasionally, a curtain would wave from one of them, blown by the draught.

They had stood outside the front door for a while, not knowing quite what to do. One or two were already making noises about going back. But then, Mrs Hingis had appeared, a broad smile across her face. She was followed shortly afterwards by her husband, carrying several large leather footballs under his arm.

'I thought we might play with these to begin with.'

He smiled as he reached the top of the steps leading up to the front door. He was wearing thin wire spectacles and from his slight, stooping figure, it seemed clear that, whatever else his skills might be, football wasn't one of them. However, he seemed keen to give it a try. Reassured by the obvious warmth of the welcome, even if a little late, the mothers said their goodbyes and turned back towards Portlecombe, leaving the children.

The day had been fun.

Before they died, each of the children spoke of the games they played, the trees they climbed, the pool they swam in. Mr Hingis had played football all morning, Mrs Hingis had taken the girls out into the nearby woods looking for flowers to press. They had stood on the cliffs and thrown stones far out into the sea. They'd been rock climbing. They'd chased rabbits. They'd had a picnic lunch under the cedar tree with all the sandwiches and lemonade they could eat and drink. And later, Mr Hingis had appeared with some tall metal hoops, some coloured balls and wooden mallets. It was called croquet and he'd said it was a game they must learn to play. It had been difficult to decide who'd been having more fun. The Hingis parents or the children.

It had been odd that Eve hadn't joined in. After all, it was supposed to have been her party. However, Mrs Hingis had explained that Eve hadn't been feeling very well. She'd been up for most of the night before and was now resting. She hoped Eve would be able to join them for tea. Occasionally, as they ran shrieking and whooping round the house, the children would glance up at the windows. Some said they had seen Eve there, standing at the window's edge, watching. She had never smiled. Or waved.

Eventually, exhausted, sweating, happy, the children had sat at the long wooden table on the lawn in front of the house. Mrs Hingis had laid it herself and it was covered with iced buns, sponge cakes, jams, scones, biscuits and large cups of cream. There was lemonade, ginger beer, some apple wine that Mrs Hingis had made and large jugs of cold orange juice. In the centre stood a large, fat, round, white cake, with a ring of candles running round the top of it.

'Is it Eve's birthday?' Lizzie had asked.

'No,' Mrs Hingis had replied. 'It's just Eve's party.'

As the children had begun to eat, they hadn't at first noticed Eve leaving the house and walking across the grass towards them. She was carrying a round, china bowl. Then they saw her and the table fell silent as the girl approached. None of the children quite knew what to say. One of them coughed, nervously. Eve stopped when she reached the table. She glanced at a boy called Harry, who was sitting at its head.

He smiled, briefly, and then stood up. 'Do you want . . . ?'

He didn't finish the question, but simply moved further down the table, leaving the chair for Eve. She walked to it slowly, putting the china bowl down in front of her. Then she looked up, the shadows of the cedar tree now stretching across the ground towards her.

'I made these for you,' she said quietly. Reaching down, she took the lid off the bowl, setting it down on the table. She looked across at her parents.

'They're only for my friends.'

Her mother nodded. Her father sat quietly, looking down at his plate.

Then Eve had carried the pot round the table, dipping a spoon inside and serving the children with its contents. Each spoonful held a large, slightly yellow-coloured mushroom, partially covered in runny, cold white sauce.

'They're called Sweet Mushrooms,' she said as she moved round.

'They're supposed to give you magic powers.' She reached the head of the table again. She smiled and sat down slowly, her gaze wandering round the faces in front of her. Nobody had spoken.

'You must eat them,' she said.

Lizzie had laughed, nervously.

'Eve, I don't like — '

'Oh, they're not like ordinary mushrooms. And you must eat them. All of you. It's my party.' Eve had smiled again.

And then Laughing Boy had started to laugh. ''Course we're going to eat them. We all want to be magic, don't we?'

And he'd laughed until the tears had rolled down his face. And the children had then started to laugh. And Eve's mother. And her father. And they'd begun to eat the mushrooms, and then more cakes and more biscuits, and by the time their mothers had arrived, four of them, walking slowly down the gravelled drive, the children had almost completely cleared the table.

Eve had picked up the empty bowl and taken it back to the house but, when the children finally began to leave, she had reappeared at the top of the front-door steps.

'Goodbye Eve!' the children had shouted. Eve had waved.

'Perhaps she's feeling better,' Mrs Hingis had murmured, but no one had heard her. They were all far too busy chasing Laughing Boy, who was running round and round the lawn, flapping his arms and waiting for the magic to turn him into a bird.

It had been a tired group of children that finally began walking back down the hill to their homes. Each one smiling, each yawning and each brimming with magic at the end of a long, hot day. As they neared the cottages of the town, the first spots of rain had begun to fall. The storm that the red skies of the morning had threatened was now about to break.

* * *

The rain had fallen hard during the evening, running from the roofs and gathering into long streams of thick, bubbling water that coursed down Portlemouth Hill and washed down the thin main street. The windows and doors of the town had been fastened tight against the wind and the unceasing curtain of rain that fell from a starless sky.

John Dornom had been the first.

Shortly before midnight, his mother, unable to sleep as the rain swept against her bedroom window, had heard him groaning, then crying out for her. Jumping from her bed, she had gone into his room to find the boy clutching his blanket tightly in his fists, his face contorted with pain, his body curled up like a snail inside its shell. She knelt by his bedside, clutching his wrist, feeling for his pulse. It was beating hard. The boy was covered in sweat, his cries of pain muffled as he pushed the blanket into his mouth.

'Edward!' His mother had shouted at her husband, who she could now hear fumbling about in the dark bedroom next door. 'Get the doctor! Now! And get me some water!'

She turned back to her son, running her hand across his forehead, holding him to her, praying. Edward Dornom had run out into the rain, slamming the door behind him. As he now peered through the darkness, he could hear shouting, could see dark shadows running.

'Hello!' he had shouted. 'Who's there?'

'That you Edward?'

'Yes, it is. Who's that?'

'Michael. Harry's dad.'

Other voices now began to shout. Anxious voices. Frightened voices. Voices of anger. Of pain. Voices that screamed in panic as the rain lashed across the rooftops and hissed off the cobbles of the street.

Voices that told the same story. Of young children who had been poisoned.

The doctor was woken from his bed, dragged half-dressed through the night from one rain-soaked house to another, from one bedside to the next, unable to understand what was going on, unable to help other than with a dose of laudanum which he had hoped might ease the pain.

* * *

The first light of the dawn had brought calm. The storm had moved away to the east. After the first, terrifying attacks, the children had each begun to recover. The fever eased, their temperatures came down, their pulse rates slowed. It might have been the laudanum. The doctor didn't think so but he said nothing.

As the day grew older, so the smiles returned, the misery of the night quickly forgotten. Families began to laugh, to swap stories of running wildly around in the storm, of bumping into each other, of how the poor old doctor must have been soaked through and through without his jacket on. The general view was that it must have been the party. Too much food. Too much running around. Too much excitement. Children never seemed to learn.

In time, bemused, almost surprised, the children themselves had begun to emerge on to the streets, to play football or to laugh and shout in a way that, only hours before, their mothers and fathers had feared they might never do again. It was as if nothing had happened. The violent nausea, the fearsome stomach cramps, the sudden difficulty in breathing. It was all quickly forgotten.

Perhaps because of their experience, the children seemed to spend the day together. They remembered the happiness of the party. They talked about the games, the exploring, the kindness of Eve's parents. They had felt sorry for Eve, sorry that she hadn't been able to join them. And they promised each other that they'd make a special effort to welcome her to school at the beginning of the next term. Annie Hannaford even said she'd have a party. Laughing Boy had said he hoped Annie wasn't doing the cooking and, watching from their cottage doorways, their parents had smiled as the children had walked by, arm in arm and laughing together in the sunlight.

They did not know it then, but it was to be the last time they would hear that laughter.

That night, the attacks returned. This time more strongly. This time the children were screaming and, in the quiet of a summer night without rain, their screams were heard through the town. By two o'clock, as the dull bell of St Peter's chimed the hour, the sound drifting slowly across the quiet, darkened waters of the harbour, the town had fallen silent once more. None could hear the private grief of mothers and fathers as they knelt at the bedsides of their children who had died.

* * *

'Deathcap,' said Phoebe slowly, her eyes quite still as her memory wandered back to days she rarely brought to mind.

'Deathcap?' said Ben.

'It's a mushroom. It looks like a mushroom. They say it even tastes like a mushroom. But it's poisonous. And there isn't a cure.'

'But the children recovered,' said Lindsay.

'For a day.' Phoebe's voice was quiet. 'That's why the Deathcap is a particularly nasty poison. It makes you ill. Lets you get better. And then it comes back and kills you.' The old woman let her head sink back against her chair. 'And they all died. All except one.'

'Laughing Boy?' said Ben.

Phoebe smiled. 'Yes, Laughing Boy. Except nobody saw him laugh again.'

'Then what happened to him? Why is his name on the wall?'

'Because he disappeared. The mushrooms might have killed the others stone dead but they got poor old Laughing Boy too. In the end. He never spoke a word after what happened that final night. It was just as if he'd been struck dumb. On the afternoon of the funerals, I can remember him just standing there up at the church, in the rain, the tears running down his face. He was in shock. In a world of his own. And then suddenly, he'd gone. Leapt over the wall and was off down the road like a rabbit. And that was the last anyone ever saw of him.'

She turned to Lindsay.

'And now you say he's still alive?'

Lindsay nodded. The old woman looked away again, into the distance. 'Then I suppose it must be him.'

Ben stood up, stretching his legs. He walked a few paces down the lawn, bending to pick up a small stick which he then threw towards the creek. It hit the water, splashing quietly. Ben watched the ripples, thoughtfully. Just a few weeks ago, Edison would have been there to retrieve it. He turned to his grandmother again.

'What happened to the girl?'

Phoebe looked up at him. Behind her, above the hills, the sun was sinking lower in the sky. It had been much the same that night, all those years ago.

* * *

They had gathered in the churchyard. Their voices were low, their conversation kept to a minimum, partly out of respect for the souls that lay beneath the ground, partly in fear of what they were about to do. In all, there had been some thirty men. Fishermen, farm workers, shopkeepers and, at their head, the headmaster, who stood on a wooden bench outside the church and looked towards the men standing in front of him, their backs to the setting sun.

To his right were two craftsmen from the stonemason's. They had made the gravestones for the children. They had also made the stone box they were now carrying.

'Does anybody want to say anything?'

The headmaster's voice was subdued. Nobody spoke.

A solitary rook floated high above the

church tower and then turned, lazily wheeling down towards the woods that lay beyond. The skies were golden as the sun edged its way toward the horizon, their brilliant light reflected in the still waters of the harbour below. No boats were moving. The town had fallen silent.

The first sounds from the road came as the church clock had begun to chime the half-hour. Half past seven. It would take an hour to reach the house, by which time the sun would have set. They came slowly through the gathering twilight that had already begun to mask the shadowed corners of the surrounding fields. Each woman carried a bundle of sticks, tied together with string. They didn't speak but walked in a column up the narrow road, their faces unsmiling, their eyes turned away from the sun.

As they entered through the small churchyard gate, they now went to stand with the men. Still, no one spoke. A dog could be heard barking, far down below in the streets of the town. In the fields to the right, a cow lowed softly. A light evening wind touched the leaves of the oak tree that stood proudly to their side, shaking them, rustling them.

The headmaster looked up, his eyes meeting those of the townspeople before him. He was silent for a moment and then slowly, he lifted his head up and closed his eyes, his face now washed in the gold of the sunset. He began to sing. 'Abide with me'. A hymn they had often sung in church. A hymn that asked for comfort, for help, for a friend with whom to face the darkness lying ahead. As the headmaster sang, so they all joined him, their voices, as one, drifting across the harbour and the hills beyond. As they finished, the headmaster once more lowered his head.

'May God be with us.'

Then they lit the torches. The tightly-bundled sticks prepared by the women, soaked in animal fat and padded with clay to slow their burning. As one, they left the churchyard, the procession of lights now visible to the surrounding hills and valleys as they made their way down towards the town.

The headmaster walked at the front. In his right hand he was carrying a cloth bag, tightly fastened at its neck. In the churchyard, it had been lying on the ground, where someone had seen it twitching. They had not asked what was inside.

They walked quickly down the hill, slowing only as they met the first houses and began their procession through the town. Those who were not going, the old and the young, now stood at their dimly-lit doorways and watched them pass by, the light from their burning torches spilling on to their faces, each face without emotion, some streaked with the burnt ash of the torches. All that was heard was the shuffle of clothing, the click of boots on the cobblestones.

At the back of each mind was fear. The belief that they were about to stare into the eyes of the very Devil himself, reincarnated in the human form of a child. The wreccan. They knew what must be done, the lessons having been handed down from the generations of long ago. But none knew what would happen. Except the headmaster.

And then they were through the small town and had started up the hill towards the cliffs. The sun had disappeared and in the deepening blue sky, small stars had begun to shine. It was colder now and the torches flickered more urgently in the strengthening wind of the evening. They reached the top of the hill. Without pausing, they now turned to the left. Very soon, the stone pillars of the gates stood in front of them. Here, they stopped. The headmaster turned towards them, his eyes glittering in the waving, dancing flames of the torches. He nodded. Then led them as they began their descent to the house. Above, the shadows danced among the branches of the trees and, at their sides, bright eyes burnt briefly in the night as small animals turned their heads to see who, or what, was going by.

Then, the house was in front of them.

For many, it was the first time they had seen it. For some, it was a return to the memories of a sunny afternoon when their children ran free. An oil-lamp was burning by the front door, its tall light flickering in occasional swirls of the wind. They began to approach the building, walking slowly now, their boots slipping on the crumbling gravel. As they grew nearer, those in front could see the silhouette of the table on the lawn. At first, it might have been a trick of the light but, as they drew closer, they could clearly see that at either end of it, there was a figure, sitting stiffly upright. Unmoving.

The headmaster stopped.

He watched the two figures carefully, then started to walk slowly towards them. A man on his right began to follow. The headmaster reached the table. In the light of the torches, waving behind him, he recognized the two people. Not many months before, he had shown them round his school. Behind him, the villagers were now beginning to move forwards, their torchlight flickering across the lawn. A man stood beside the headmaster, his torch held high. His son, Harry, had been at the party.

'The parents?' The headmaster nodded. 'Are they . . . ?'

'Yes, I'm afraid so. Quite dead.'

The light of the gathered torches illuminated the front of the house, the glass of the tall windows reflecting the people standing below.

It was at one of the upper windows that the girl now appeared, a hideous grin stretched across her face, her eyes opened wide and seeming to stare into the very hearts of those who now looked up at her. She began to shake, her body contorting, twisting, her head flung back as she screamed and then began to laugh. A shrill, ear-splitting, shrieking sound that echoed through the empty rooms and through the very bricks of the house itself.

'Witch!'

Harry's father ran forward, howling the word over and over again at the demonic figure that now seemed to be dancing against the window, dancing with joy and in contempt of the people below. Reaching the house, he paused briefly and then, screaming, hurled his torch through one of the lower windows. The glass shattered. Inside, the torch broke against the floor, cascading sparks across the room. As he fell to his knees, another villager ran forwards. Again, a window was broken, again torch flames licked hungrily at the wooden floors and soft carpets.

Now shouting, screaming, shrieking, the crowd surged forwards. As the piercing howls of laughter still came from inside, they mixed with the sound of breaking glass and the increasing roar of the flames as the lower rooms of the house began to burn.

Within minutes, the entire house was alight, a giant torch against the night-time sky whose flames leapt towards the stars and whose heat scorched the skins of the villagers as they stood back and watched in awe and in horror. The upper floors were enveloped, the hideous laughter had ceased. All that was now to be heard was the crack of splitting timber, the rumble of falling bricks and the greedy howl of the flames as they savaged the building and scraped the life from its carcass.

It was with the flames at their height that the girl appeared.

Emerging from the fiery hell behind her, she was now standing at the top of the steps, her body, her clothes, her face untouched by the inferno. Still, the smile was on her face, the lips slightly parted, the teeth glittering behind.

The crowd had fallen silent. Their words, their shouting, their screaming now cloying, drying in their throats. They watched without speaking as the girl began to walk down the steps. Slowly, her white dress trailing on the stone. Her eyes blazed as she stared at the people before her. As she reached the edge of the lawn, she stopped and once more began to shake her body, rolling her head from side to side, moaning.

The headmaster stepped forwards.

Quite deliberately, without fear, he walked towards the grotesque figure. As if in a trance, she appeared not to notice him, her moaning now a constant wail, interrupted only by short, high-pitched laughter. In his hand, the headmaster still held the cloth bag but the string that had tied its neck was undone, its contents now held in place only by the man's fingers curled about its top. He reached the girl, standing quite still before her.

Still the crowd were silent. Still the flames reached high into the air as the house gradually disintegrated. And then the girl stopped. Her head quite still, she stared at the headmaster, looked at her own reflection in his eyes, her pale face framed by the fires behind her.

Quite suddenly, the headmaster grabbed her wrist and, fumbling for the bag, forced her hand deep inside it, holding it there, tightly.

The bag seemed to writhe, seemed to leap, seemed to curl about the girl's arm. Almost as if it had come to life and was now clawing the flesh from her bones. The girl screamed. Her wide mouth now open as she shrieked from the very corners of her soul. She threw her body from side to side, kicked, spat, lashed at the headmaster's face with her other hand, her nails tearing wide, bloody slits across his face. But still he held her hand in the bag, staring hard into her deep, black eyes. And then, the girl had suddenly stiffened. Her eyes were wide, her face twisted almost as if in shock. She was perfectly still and then, slowly, noiselessly, slumped to the ground. The headmaster took her hand from the bag and then turned, tied its neck, and flung it far into the night.

'Now!' he shouted, glancing across at the crowd, searching for the two stone-masons. 'We don't have long.'

The two men came forward, breathing heavily, struggling to carry the stone box they held between them.

'We'll need more of you!' shouted the headmaster. 'And we'll need light. Quickly!'

The stonemasons reached the fallen body of the girl. They put the box on the lawn, carefully removing the lid. They tried not to look at the girl, her face still frozen, her eyes still gazing, sightless, ahead of her.

'Take her feet!'

The headmaster's voice was urgent. He knew there was little time left. The men hesitated, neither wanting to touch the girl lying on the ground. 'Now!' The headmaster grasped the girl under the arms, lifting the upper half of her body. Her head fell to one side, her mouth open. One of the men, seeing the rows of teeth for the first time, felt the bile rising in his throat. He turned quickly away. The other, now helped by Harry's father, grabbed the girl's legs and with the headmaster, they carried the girl to the cold stone box and gently laid her in it. The girl's eyes flickered.

'The lid!' The headmaster was suddenly shouting. He could see the girl's mouth now beginning to twist. Her head was turning, twitching. 'For pity's sake!'

The men had the lid. It was in the air. Suddenly the girl was staring at the headmaster, the hate in her eyes so livid that it burnt into the fibres of his brain. From the depths of her throat, she began to hiss, her arms to shiver.

And then she was blinded as the lid fell in place and total darkness now folded over her. Against the flames of the house, the headmaster now stood back, staring at the stone coffin, silent as a rescued soul, drawn back from the edges of Hell.

* * *

The procession to the cliff top was slow. The house fires were burning out but there was light enough for the villagers to see their way to the outcrop. Again, the headmaster was leading, followed by four men who carried the girl's coffin. One or two of the crowd still held torches. Others held small candle lamps.

Reaching the edges of the cliff, they stopped. The headmaster turned, his back now to the sea, the breeze that blew off it pulling at the long, greying strands of his hair.

'She is going now,' he said.

'Damn her!' shouted a voice from the crowd. 'Damn her to Hell!'

'And pray to God that she never comes back.'

A villager stepped forward and offered him a lamp. 'Leave it down there. Someone might need it one day.'

The headmaster nodded and took it, turning back to face the rocky outcrop, its outline stark against the breaking waves of the sea. Lifting the lamp, he could see the crack in the rock and he walked to it, followed by the men carrying the coffin and those who carried torches. The girl would lie in the caves down below, undisturbed by the centuries to come, her spirit held in place by a stone lid, bearing the mark of the snake.

* * *

The evening breeze was now cold. Too cold for the old woman who had struggled up from her garden chair and was now turning back towards her cottage. Ben took her arm, helping her.

'And yet she's back,' said Phoebe, stopping and turning to Lindsay. 'I told your grandfather, I knew she'd be back for us.'

'Us?' said Lindsay.

'The three of us who didn't go to the party. I knew she'd be back. One day.'

Lindsay could see the fear in the old woman's eyes. She moved to her, taking her other arm. 'Then we'll have to make sure she doesn't get any of you,' she said softly.

Ben's mind had gone back to the

picture hanging in the museum. 1937. The girl, the two boys. The survivors, their faces grim, their eyes sad.

'Who were they?' he said.

'Who?'

'The two boys.'

Phoebe looked at him for a moment. He had the same blue eyes as Donald. The same proud forehead.

'Your grandfather was one,' she said. And then turned to Lindsay. 'And yours was the other.'

The three of them walked up the short garden towards the cottage, while behind them the waters of the creek lapped gently along the shoreline.

Later, as he poured water into the kettle, Ben looked out of the kitchen window, gazing at the early evening shadows of the garden, remembering the storm, the dog, the face at the window.

'Maybe Talleyard's right,' he said, glancing at the reflection in the window of his grandmother and Lindsay, sitting at the kitchen table. 'Maybe we're all dreaming. Maybe what we've seen is all no more than an illusion.'

'Well,' said Phoebe, thoughtfully. 'He would know.'

'Why?'

The old woman looked up. 'His father was the headmaster.'

* * *

There was no one at home.

Lindsay thought it odd. But nothing more. By seven o'clock, her grandfather would normally have been in the kitchen, cooking, a glass of cider on the table and the smell of bubbling, fresh vegetables drifting through to the hall.

Now, the cottage was empty. There was no note of explanation in the hall. No brief scribbled mention of a glass of beer with friends in the Victoria Inn. Or of an evening stroll along the cliffs. She closed the front door behind her, instinctively reaching for the light switch to her left. Sinking behind the cliffs at last, the sun had left the town and its harbour and already the evening was growing dark. She went through to the kitchen. Everything was in its place. The windows were closed, the curtains still pulled back.

She took a glass from the cupboard and walked over to the fridge. She opened it, pulling a bottle of cold spring water from the rack. Apart from the low hum of the fridge, and the predictable, slow ticking of the clock on the wall, there was no sound. She poured the water, watching the bubbles rise up the sides of the glass, only to burst at the top. She lifted the glass to her mouth, drinking deeply, the cold, sparkling water briefly stilling the worried thought that had begun to chip at the edges of her brain.

There was no note. But what was a note? Words. Simple words.

She thought again of the fireside, of her grandfather speaking softly. '*You'd remember these simple words?*' That's why there hadn't been a note. He'd already said goodbye.

She put the glass down on the table, suddenly breathing hard. Outside, the gate clicked. Moments later, someone was knocking on the front door. Pushing her chair back, suddenly, carelessly, she walked quickly from the kitchen. She opened the door.

'Ben, I — '

'They've gone. Those two old fools have gone.' Ben had been running. He was struggling to speak, 'My mum didn't understand. She said she saw them walking up the main street, about an hour ago. She asked them where they were going.' He paused, taking a long, deep breath. 'Do you know what they said?'

Lindsay knew the answer. She didn't want to ask the question.

'Where?'

The word was whispered. Ben looked at her steadily.

'Linds, they said they were going to a party.'

15

The two men stood by the oak tree, apparently looking out over the harbour, the estuary and the sea beyond but, in the peace of that late summer evening, both men knew they were looking back over their lives.

The thin, red cusp of the sun could still just be seen as it slipped below the skyline. They both knew it was time to go. Yet neither moved.

Slowly, the old song came back to Donald. The hymn the villagers had sung all those years ago when they had gathered in this churchyard, beneath this oak tree, surrounded by these graves. As a child, he had leant out of his bedroom window and heard the low chorus as the flames of the torches had threaded their way down the darkening hillside.

'Abide with me, fast falls the eventide . . . ' He sang the words slowly, his eyes still fixed on the setting sun, his face bathed in the rich glow of its closing moments. 'The darkness deepens, Lord with me abide . . . '

Now Tom began to sing and their two voices lifted into the air and mingled with the voices of the natural world as it settled for the evening. High above, a line of geese flew through the wispy, golden touches of cloud, tracing a giant letter V against the sky. Their familiar honking calls might have been goodbye.

'When other helpers fail and comforts flee, Help of the helpless, O abide with me.'

The song was finished. They knew no more. The cusp of the sun had finally gone and the familiar patterns of the day were now grown old. Without speaking, the two men looked at each other, took the other's hand and shook it. And, with tears in their eyes, they left the churchyard and began their walk to the party.

* * *

It was still light when they reached the house. Almost as if the sun had been so bright during the day that it had scarred the heavens with a light that would now fade only very slowly. There was no sign of the girl. The tangle of the garden might have concealed a thousand demons but the bushes and grasses simply blew backwards and forwards in the wind, neither saying hello nor waving goodbye.

As they stood on the edge of the lawn, Tom thought he might have heard laughter. Not the hideous, chilling laughter of the girl, but the laughter of children playing. Running carelessly, recklessly, across the gardens. Swinging from the trees. Hurling themselves into feverish and excited acrobatics, tumbling and twisting in cartwheels across the grass. The sound of the tea-party. The clatter of plates, the jangle of cutlery, the high-pitched squeals of delight at the prospect of more cake. And then, the sudden sound of silence. As the chatter and the bubbling and chuckling dies, the cold figure of Death approaches.

'So. You came.'

Tom and Donald turned quickly. Beside them stood the girl. Her hands together, her head leaning slightly to the right, her black eyes watching the two men closely.

'I'm glad you came. I missed you last time.'

'Yes. We came,' said Tom.

The girl hissed softly. Almost as if she

did not want them to speak. Donald took a step forward. 'But we want you to leave our families alone.'

'Where's the girl? There were three of you.'

'She's ill, Eve. Very ill. You must leave Phoebe alone as well.'

The girl hissed more sharply. And then spat at him. Donald didn't move.

'I do what I want,' she said, her voice thickened by the phlegm at the back of her throat. 'And anyway, she's dying now.'

Her arms were raised, almost as if she was about to start beating them against her sides like a carrion crow preparing to leave a field. Her face was thin, her teeth now glittering, standing in tight rows as she slowly opened her mouth.

'The food is ready.'

Tom glanced at Donald. His friend was shaking. He put out his hand, grasping the other man's and holding it firmly.

'Don't worry, Donald,' he whispered. 'It will be over soon.'

The girl had turned away and was now walking back towards the house. The two men began to follow.

'No,' she said, without looking back. 'Stay there. Before we eat, we play games.

That's what we did last time. It's more fun that way.'

Tom and Donald stopped. They stood quite still, watching as the girl walked through the gaping hole of the front door and then disappeared into the ruins of the house.

'Where's she gone?'

'I don't know,' said Tom.

Inside the house, its roof open to the darkening sky, a small fire burned in the hearth. At its side, a heavy china bowl sat on top of some fallen bricks, placed there to keep its contents warm. Some metres away, towards the back wall of the house, stood a charred, splintered table, on which there stood a pile of dirty plates and some rusting spoons. It was placed there because, as the light faded and the stars came out, the moonlight would fall on that corner.

Outside, the old men waited. Tom tightened the scarf around his neck. He wondered if Lindsay would remember him in the years to come.

* * *

'What are they doing?'

Ben crouched low in the bushes that

sprawled along the edges of the gardens. The trees above them swayed in the wind that blew in from the sea. 'I don't know,' he said. 'They seem to be waiting for someone.'

Lindsay knelt beside him. 'Is she there?'

'I don't think so.'

They were some two hundred metres from the house, protected by the thick brambles and by the deepening gloom of the woods around them. Nearby, a small squirrel scratched its way across the thick carpet of leaves.

'What do we do now?'

'I suppose we just wait.'

The squirrel stopped at the sound of the voices, only scrabbling its way forwards again when, after some moments, it decided that the danger had gone. It had not seen the shadow of the figure waiting further back, in the silence of the trees. The girl came out of the house. In her hands, she held what looked like a large ball.

'They used this,' she said, throwing it down on to the grass.

Neither Tom nor Donald moved. The ball rolled slowly across the lawn, stopping short of them. The light was now beginning to fade.

'Go on,' said the girl. 'Play with it.'

'Play with it?' said Tom.

'That's what they did.'

'And if we do?'

'Then we'll have tea.'

'And then what?'

The girl stared at him, her eyes unblinking.

'And then what, Eve? If we have tea, will it mean the party's over? You'll have got us all then, Eve. Won't you? Every kid in the class. Does that mean it's over?'

The girl said nothing. She simply stared at him, her long, thin red hair moving slightly with the wind.

'Speak, damn you! Say something!'

Donald was shaking his fist at her, his face contorted with fury and with terror. The girl remained motionless, waiting for him to finish, to grow quiet again. She looked forward to hearing him scream when he'd eaten his meal. Donald dropped his arm to his side, stepping back again, his shoulders slumping. In the distance, a gull called as it drifted through the twilight sky.

'Play!' The girl spat the word at them.

* * *

'I don't believe it,' said Lindsay.

'No,' said Ben, softly. 'Nor do I.'

They watched as Tom and Donald began to kick the ball to each other. The girl clapped, her shrill laughter stabbing into the silent gardens.

'How did you know?'

Neither Lindsay nor Ben moved at first. The voice was behind them. It was one they recognized.

'Whatever you do, don't move too quickly. She probably knows you're here already.' The figure remained in the shadows of the trees and, as Ben turned his head slowly round, all he could see was the dim outline of a man.

'Talleyard?'

'You haven't answered my question.'

Talleyard's voice was low. On the lawn, he could see that all three figures were still there.

'My Gran told us,' said Ben.

'Then she's a fool.'

'It was her story to tell. You said so yourself.'

Eve's shrieking laugh pealed again through the air. And still Tom and Donald kicked the ball, backwards and forwards.

'And did she also tell you why those two fools are out there?'

'No.'

'They think that if they sacrifice themselves, then that creature will go away.' Talleyard grunted. 'Idiots. The wreccan never goes away. But they have one chance.'

Talleyard knew that the girl would tire of the game soon. He had little time left. He also knew that her senses would have told her that someone was in the woods, watching. Staying in the shadows, he spoke softly again.

'Give me five minutes. No more. Then get up and walk away, back through here, past these trees, and then follow the path. When you get to the gate, wait for me.'

'Why . . .?'

'Don't ask. Just do it.'

Talleyard's outline faded into the darkness of the trees. He had five minutes to reach the house before Ben and Lindsay tripped over the dead branches he had carefully laid on the path.

⋆ ⋆ ⋆

'It'll make you very hungry,' said the girl, clapping again as Tom pushed the ball across the grass with his foot.

'Eve, why . . . ?'

Donald bent down and caught the ball in his hands as it rolled towards him. He lifted it up, holding it as if to throw it. 'Tom, there's no point in asking her anything. She wouldn't — ' Without warning, he suddenly hurled the heavy leather football at the girl. She didn't move.

The ball hammered into her face. And then bounced to the ground, leaving the girl still standing, her mouth open, her teeth spread wide. On the ground, the ball began to deflate, the air hissing out of its lacerated side.

'That was funny,' said the girl. 'But now what shall we play?'

At that moment, she heard the sharp crack of the breaking branch. She had known someone was out there, and now she knew where.

* * *

Lindsay turned to Ben in the half-light.

'Are you all right?'

'I'm sorry,' whispered Ben. 'I didn't see it.'

He was now beside Lindsay. In front, they could just see the outline of a thin track that looked as if it was running downhill through the trees, away from the house.

'I don't see why — '

'I think we should do what he says,' said Lindsay. 'I don't know where he's going or what he's doing. But he does seem to know more than we do.'

They carried on, slowly feeling their way through the darkness. Occasional openings in the branches high above their heads showed them the early evening stars. Around them, the woodland was beginning to come to life with the sounds of night-time. The owls calling. The stoat scampering across the fallen leaves. The sudden flight of a wood-pigeon disturbed by the sharp-toothed fox. They had been walking for some minutes, when Lindsay suddenly stopped.

'Ben.'

'Yes?'

'Ben. There's someone there.' Lindsay's voice was hurried.

'Where?'

'Look.' Further down the path, a faint

glow had appeared behind a tall chestnut tree, as if someone was perhaps hiding behind it with a lantern.

Ben smiled. 'It's Talleyard.'

'I thought he said something about a gate.'

'He did,' said Ben. 'And there it is.' In the faint glow ahead, they could just make out the skeleton of a wooden field-gate. 'I wonder if they're with him?'

They walked more quickly now, their steps more certain as they approached the tree. The light grew stronger. It hadn't moved. Clearly, Talleyard hadn't heard them coming.

Ben reached the tree first, leaning round it, the smile broad across his face. 'Talleyard, I . . .'

The girl smiled, the ghostly light that wreathed her in bleak contrast with the blackness of her eyes and the deep red of her hair that fell across thin, pointed cheekbones.

'So,' she said slowly, still smiling. Ben could feel the warm, damp texture of her breath on the still night air. 'You want to come to my party too.'

* * *

Talleyard could see the two men standing on the lawn. He couldn't see the girl. He didn't know how much time he had.

Standing at the back of the house and looking through the window frame, he could see the fire and the pot beside it. The table, the broken chairs around it. Pulling himself up, he clambered through the open frame. Once inside, he reached down and caught the leather strap of the basket he had left beneath the window. He pulled it up, slowly, trying not to bump it against the wall. He set it down on the floor.

He glanced towards the lawns again. Still the old men were standing there, one now shivering. Above him, he could hear a small bat flying in and out of the broken eaves of the house. Carefully, he picked his way across the broken floorboards. His boots were rubber-soled. He made little noise.

Now, as he picked up the white china pot, he could hear the old men talking in low, muted tones. He couldn't hear the words but he could hear the fear in their voices. He moved back across the room, his every sense alive to the return of the girl. He reached the window and, lifting the lid from the pot, he now poured its contents out on to the thick grass outside. A thick, pungent liquid that drained from the pot, its smell sweet, its taste almost certainly fatal.

Once emptied, he set the pot on the floor. He could feel his heart pumping hard. Carefully, he opened the basket he had brought. There was no immediate movement. He now had seconds to complete his move before the element of surprise had gone.

He flung the top wide open, grabbed the basket and quickly tipped it upside down over the empty pot. Its contents fell inside. He heard the noise as they fell against the white china. Then, as his left hand pulled the basket away, his right closed on the lid of the cooking-pot and clamped it firmly back in position. He leant back, wiping the sweat from his forehead with the sleeve of his jacket. He stood up, picked up the china pot and moved carefully back to the fire, setting the pot down again at its side. And then, quietly, he left, picking up the empty basket, climbing through the window frame and dropping slowly on to the grass outside.

* * *

Lindsay clung to her grandfather's arm. She wanted to be brave for him but suddenly, she had reached her own breaking-point. All she wanted to do was run screaming from the house. Her grandfather was sitting upright, his face lit by the moonlight that now streamed through the open roof. At the other side of the table sat Donald, his arm around Ben's shoulders. Nobody spoke.

At the far side of the room, the girl was standing by one of the tall windows that looked out over the lawns. She had been there for several minutes. By the hearth-side, the small fire continued to glow, warming the pot beside it.

Sick with the misery of what was happening, Lindsay could barely bring herself to believe that within minutes, they would be eating whatever was inside. And that within two days, they would all have died in the most vicious, painful way. She began to cry, her sobbing reaching down to the very bottom of her heart. Her grandfather turned, taking her in his arms, hugging her close to him, pressing her face into his shoulder.

Eve turned, grinning. 'Teatime,' she said.

Gingerly, almost on tip-toe, she began to cross the room towards the fire. Donald and Ben sat with their backs to her, refusing to watch what she might be doing. But they could hear. Hear the soft giggling as the girl picked up the pot. The fall of her shoes on the rotted floorboards as she began to move to the table. Still they refused to look, staring fixedly out at the night skies beyond.

Eve reached the table, gently putting the pot down in front of her.

'Well, don't you want a plate? We always have plates. It's polite.'

She walked round the table, putting a plate down in front of each person. Lindsay clung to her grandfather. Tom held her, his eyes following Eve as she moved round the group. Donald continued to stare out of the window.

'I'm not hungry,' said Ben.

'You will be,' said the girl, putting a plate in front of him. She sat at the head of the table, the plates served, the white pot in front of her. She looked up.

'Shall I be mother?'

Then she threw back her head, letting

her long, red hair trail to the floor as she laughed, her hands clinging to the table as her whole body shook, the sweat pouring down the sides of her neck. Suddenly, she was sitting upright again, her hands tightening on the sides of the pot, a spoon in one of them.

Now each person at the table was watching her. She grinned. 'I hope you enjoy it.'

She lifted the lid.

Sealed in the pot, left by the fireside, cramped and scalded, the snakes were blind with fury. As she opened the pot, they sprang viciously from it, their movement almost too quick to follow, their dark, patterned bodies wriggling as they reached for her. They clung to her neck, opening their mouths and sinking their fangs deep into her skin. Again and again, they struck, their small heads darting in and out. Eve was screaming, shrieking, howling, her eyes wide in terror, her body stiffening. As the adders at last fell from her and disappeared into the shadows, she slid slowly from her chair and fell to the dirty floor below.

The silence was broken only by the sound of the small bat still haunting the charred edges of the roof above, looking for small insects in the light of the moon.

Talleyard's face appeared at the open window.

'We have very little time.'

* * *

Tom led the way, running across the uneven heather, the torch Lindsay was carrying flickering across the ground in front of him. Ben and his grandfather carried the girl.

Ahead, they could hear the sea, the rolling waves pulling gently at the rocks.

'Quickly!' said Talleyard, glancing anxiously at Eve.

'We're there.' Tom stopped beside the outcrop of rock. The crack in its side was still visible, the brambles and weeds left broken and pulled to one side.

'I'll go first.'

Lindsay's words weren't a suggestion. She was simply saying what was happening. She clambered in through the crack, her torch illuminating the space beyond. Tom followed. Then Ben, his grandfather, the prone body of the girl. Talleyard held his lantern high, its light always spilling on to the girl's face. His eyes were watching for the first signs of movement.

They began the curling, shadowed descent into the caves. The air grew colder, the smell of the water below reaching up the tunnels towards them. Their feet slipped on the shale. Their hands and arms were bloodied by the constant buffeting against the rock sides. They tumbled, they fell, they slid, they collided with each other and still they were going down. Still the girl's eyes remained fixed. Black. Empty.

Talleyard glanced at his watch. There could be very little time left.

And then, suddenly, they were on level ground. As Lindsay spun the torch beam into the air around her, they could see the tall, rounded sides of the cave.

'The coffin!' shouted Talleyard. 'Find the coffin!'

Lindsay swept the beam across the floor. The stone coffin was caught in the pale yellow light. It was open. Ben and his grandfather glanced at each other and then, sweating, began to work their way across the room, carrying, half-dragging the girl.

'Oh no!'

Talleyard was shouting. He had seen the eyes flicker.

'Come on!'

Tom turned, grabbing the girl's feet, and now three of them bundled her across the room towards the coffin.

'Keep the light on the coffin!'

Lindsay was standing with her back to the pool, trying to keep the beam steady in her shaking hand. Eve's eyes were widening now.

They reached the coffin, Tom breaking away to go to its other side. They began to lift the girl. Still her eyes widened, and now began to roll. Her lips were beginning to part.

'Keep the light still!'

Behind her, the waters of the pool began to boil. Lindsay couldn't look, dared not look. She stared at the coffin, her hands shaking violently as she struggled to keep the torch beam on it. Behind her, the eel rose from the water.

They threw the girl into the coffin, bundling her on to her back.

The eel climbed through the air. As it did, so Eve's eyes followed it, a smile broadening on her face.

Talleyard stared wildly about him.

'The lid!'

From the coffin, Eve was now beginning to scream with delight.

The eel's mouth opened as it towered above the group on the platform, its deep black eyes fixed on the girl with the light. It began to fall.

'Lindsay!'

Ben threw himself across the floor, hurling himself against Lindsay, hammering her against the far wall. To the sound of a scream that would forever be in their ears, Tom and Donald buckled and fell with the stone lid, crashing it into place on top of the coffin. Shaking, gasping, clutching for breath, they lay on the floor of the cave, as the eel sank slowly back into the depths.

16

Phoebe had wanted to be there. In fact, she had said it was her duty. No one else could do it. They'd tried to tell her it wasn't an easy walk. But Phoebe had been determined. And so it was that Ben and Lindsay found themselves walking down the quiet lane past the church with Phoebe as the sun climbed high into the August sky.

'Grandad said it was a kind of sacrifice,' said Ben. 'That's why they did it. To stop her hurting the rest of us.'

'Do you think it would have stopped her?' Lindsay paused as they neared the small wooden field-gate.

'No,' said Phoebe. 'Nothing would have stopped her.'

'Then they were very brave.'

Phoebe carefully opened the gate.

'No,' she said, slowly. 'They were fools.'

They began to walk across the long, thick grass of the field. Further down, the cows seemed unconcerned.

'Gran,' said Ben. 'How come Talleyard knew so much?'

'His father,' said Phoebe. 'He might have earned his living as a headmaster but he was a countryman at heart. There wasn't much he didn't know about the land. All this.'

She stopped and looked across the fields, the woods, the hills and the valleys that surrounded the small harbour in the distance.

'There was a time when we knew what we were doing in this world.'

She shook her head, thinking of how much had been lost, so quickly. The old ways, the old customs, the old knowledge. Now buried deep in the earth, along with the thousands that lay buried on the battlefields of Europe, her husband among them.

'But not any more.' Phoebe looked up again. 'The headmaster knew what to do. But he always blamed himself for what happened. Always said that he should have realized sooner what the girl was. He'd spent his life collecting country lore. He'd known the stories about the wreccan. He should have recognized her. And yet it had been he, the headmaster, who had persuaded the parents to let the children go to the party. He never forgave himself.

That's why they found him hanging in his kitchen a few years later.'

'And he taught everything he knew to his son?' said Lindsay.

'I suppose it was in case she should ever come back,' said Phoebe. 'And she did.'

They had reached the top of the hill and were looking down towards the creek below.

'Will you help me down?' said Phoebe quietly.

Carefully, they helped the old woman down the slope, the thick, red Devon soil rutted and pot-holed by the work of rabbits over the years. Thin tracks worn by the hooves of sheep criss-crossed their path. Finally, they stood at the edge of the creek, looking across to the small shingle beach at the far side. There was no one to be seen, although a thin wisp of smoke was climbing from the small stick fire.

'Follow me,' said Lindsay, remembering how she had first been shown the way. They walked round the creek, its still waters providing a playground for large, shimmering dragonflies. Small black insects crawled across wide, floating leaves. Occasionally, a fish would rise, its mouth pouting above the water before once more letting it close above its head. They reached the beach.

'Hello?' Phoebe called softly. 'Is anyone here?'

A crow called from the trees above, repeatedly, its raucous chant as if in answer to the old woman. Phoebe walked forward, her shoes crunching lightly on the shingle. Ben was about to follow. Lindsay stopped him, holding out her arm. Phoebe walked on, pausing by the small fire, enjoying the smell of the wood-smoke. It was the wood of an apple tree. Always the best. Now she looked up towards the cave. Tears had begun to well at the back of her eyes. The curtain, hanging in front of the cave, moved slightly.

'Hello?' Phoebe called again. As she watched, so a figure appeared, pulling the curtain slowly to one side. He wore a fisherman's cap. A long dark coat. Baggy trousers flapped about the top of his boots. Long, greying hair fell to his shoulders. He saw Phoebe.

'Laughing Boy?' she called. 'Is that you?'

The man stood for a moment, the silence broken only by the gentle ripples of the estuary as its waters brushed against the shingle. 'Is it really you?'

Then Laughing Boy smiled. A smile that grew broader and broader. Until, suddenly, he was laughing. A laugh that curled back over the years and was once more the laughter of a child among children, running, dancing and singing in the summer sun.

He began to walk forwards. And then to stumble and to run, until finally he was hugging Phoebe, the tears rolling down his cheeks, his laughter buried in the warmth and comfort of her arms as she held someone she had thought she would never see again. At last, they looked at each other, as the sunlight filtered through the trees and through the smoke of the apple-wood.

'Come on, Laughing Boy,' she said softly. 'It's time to come home.'

We do hope that you have enjoyed reading this large print book.

Did you know that all of our titles are available for purchase?

We publish a wide range of high quality large print books including:
Romances, Mysteries, Classics
General Fiction
Non Fiction and Westerns

Special interest titles available in large print are:
The Little Oxford Dictionary
Music Book, Song Book
Hymn Book, Service Book

Also available from us courtesy of Oxford University Press:
Young Readers' Dictionary
(large print edition)
Young Readers' Thesaurus
(large print edition)

For further information or a free brochure, please contact us at:
Ulverscroft Large Print Books Ltd.,
The Green, Bradgate Road, Anstey,
Leicester, LE7 7FU, England.
Tel: (00 44) **0116 236 4325**
Fax: (00 44) **0116 234 0205**

Other titles in the
Spectrum Imprint:

AT GEHENNA'S DOOR

Peter Beere

Hiking across open moor can be dangerous, especially during a storm. But for four intrepid walkers, the weather is the least of their worries . . . Lost, cold and wet, Caroline and her friends stumble upon an old house hidden in the mists. Gehenna — place of torment. It doesn't look very inviting and Franklin, the owner, is the stuff of nightmares. But it is only a halfway house, after all. It's not as if Gehenna will turn out to be their final resting place — will it?

Point CRIME

THE SECRETS OF THE DEAD

Malcolm Rose

LAWLESS:

Brett. Detective Inspector with a lot to prove. Biochemical background. Hot on analysis but prone to wild theories. Dangerous.

TILLEY:

Clare. Detective Sergeant with her feet on the ground. Tough and intuitive. Completely sane. She needs to be.

THE CASE:

Four bodies have been found in the Peak District. They're rotting fast and vital evidence needs to be taken from the corpses. You need a strong stomach to work in Forensics . . . Brett's got a theory, but it could cost him his job. He's going to pursue it anyway . . .

Point R♥mance

ICE HOT!

Robyn Turner

Jackie's boyfriend Julian seems too busy to see her these days. So when she's offered free entry to the local ice-rink, she thinks it's the perfect way to fill her spare time. Soon the ice is sizzling and Jackie discovers there's much, much more to life than Julian. The skating teacher, Adam, is the most gorgeous man she's ever seen. And if Vikram's just a good friend, why can't she keep her eyes off him? The ice-rink may be a chilly place to hang out, but it's looking pretty hot right now . . .

FOOTBALL FANATIC

Rob Childs

Luke Crawford is totally soccer mad. Trouble is, his encyclopaedic, anorak-type knowledge of the game is not matched by his ball skills on the pitch. Appearances for the school team are rare, but Luke realizes there is a way to guarantee himself a regular game of footie. He can form his own team to play in the Sunday League, and then he can pick himself to play centre-forward every single week! All he needs is ten more players . . .

GIRLS UNDER PRESSURE

Jacqueline Wilson

I think I look awful — horribly hugely F-A-T. My friends Magda and Nadine think I'm mad — but it's all right for them. Magda looks drop-dead gorgeous (though boys always get the wrong idea about her). Nadine's got model looks — and a chance to be a cover girl! But I'm a real Ellie the Elephant, so I'm going on a serious diet. And this time I'm going to stick to it, no matter what . . .

In this moving and funny sequel to GIRLS IN LOVE, Ellie, Magda and Nadine all try to change their looks — with drastic consequences. These girls are under pressure!

THE VANISHED

Celia Rees

It all started as stories — playground tales handed down for generations. Stories of plague graves, vanished children and hidden steps leading to a festering underworld. A world so real you could almost smell it . . . But when another child goes missing, Fraser wonders if there's some truth in the tales. The dank tunnels running under the city are real enough. Who knows what horrors their depths contain? Only Billy. He knows about a decaying kingdom far more terrifying than anyone could imagine . . .

3 8002 02261 866 6

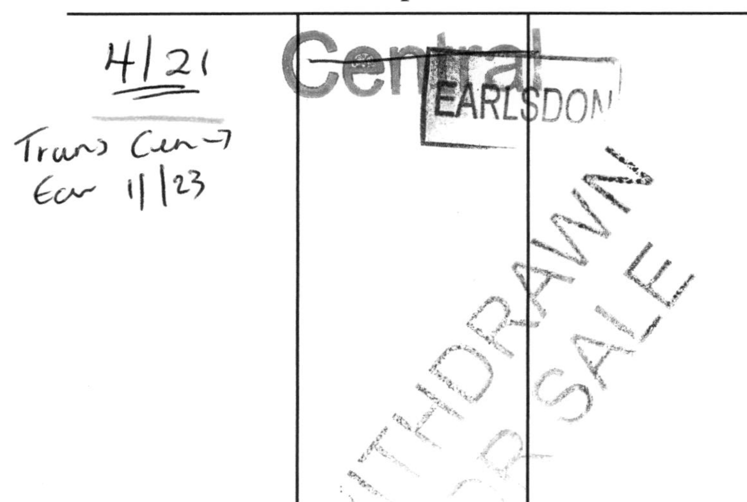
4/21
Trans Cen → Ear 1/23
Central
EARLSDON
WITHDRAWN FOR SALE

SPECIAL MESSAGE TO READERS

This book is published under the auspices of

THE ULVERSCROFT FOUNDATION

(registered charity No. 264873 UK)

Established in 1972 to provide funds for research, diagnosis and treatment of eye diseases. Examples of contributions made are: —

A Children's Assessment Unit at Moorfield's Hospital, London.

•

Twin operating theatres at the Western Ophthalmic Hospital, London.

•

A Chair of Ophthalmology at the Royal Australian College of Ophthalmologists.

•

The Ulverscroft Children's Eye Unit at the Great Ormond Street Hospital For Sick Children, London.

You can help further the work of the Foundation by making a donation or leaving a legacy. Every contribution, no matter how small, is received with gratitude. Please write for details to:

THE ULVERSCROFT FOUNDATION,
The Green, Bradgate Road, Anstey,
Leicester LE7 7FU, England.
Telephone: (0116) 236 4325

In Australia write to:
THE ULVERSCROFT FOUNDATION,
c/o The Royal Australian College of Ophthalmologists,
27, Commonwealth Street, Sydney, N.S.W. 2010.